RAY OF LIGHT

ELIZABETH JOHNS

RAY OF LIGHT

ELIZABETH JOHNS

Cover Design by Wilette Youkey
Edited by Tessa Shapcott
Historical consultant Heather King

ISBN-13: 978-0-9965754-7-8

CHAPTER 1

all, dark and handsome, and about as warm as a dead fish. Maili Craig wondered why the Duke of Cavenray had even asked her to dance—a waltz no less—when it seemed he had no intention of attempting even polite civilities. At least he smelled better than a dead fish, she decided, as she detected his scent of cloves and spice.

Perhaps if she closed her eyes, she could be more charitable. He did feel very nice, and his height was enough not to make her feel like a maypole towering over the other ladies. However, the Duke was the one person she felt most anxious about when near, which was silly since her uncle Yardley was a duke. But something in Cavenray's eyes spoke of disapproval and it put her on the defensive. The knowledge disturbed her; she knew it, yet could not muster enough grace to overcome it.

Thankfully, he could not detect her sweaty palms beneath her gloves. Under normal circumstances, she would have chatted the dance away as she was prone to let her tongue run on when she was nervous—and she was very, very nervous. This was the first time he had asked her to dance, and she could not fathom why.

Speaking of fish, Maili had been feeling like a fish out of water without Christelle alongside her since her cousin had married and departed for Scotland. The Sefton ball was the last entertainment left on the family's social calendar before leaving for the country. The Season had lost its lustre, and the usual court of admirers seemed more reluctant to shower attention on her without Christelle present —a lowering thought. Cavenray had frequently been amongst those gentlemen seen paying homage to Christelle and herself. These last few weeks of the Season had been lonely, and Maili feared she had lost her opportunity to make a match.

It was no secret the Duke had been courting Christelle, who had chosen a mere physician—her brother Seamus—instead. To be sure, he was an earl now, but he had not been when Christelle had fallen in love with him. Maili sighed as she thought longingly about marrying for true love herself. She had dreamed about coming to London and having a Season for as long as she could remember. Her sister, Catriona, had tried to warn her not to get her hopes up or look too high for a husband, or she would be disappointed.

She had, of course, taken Catriona's words as a challenge.

She was dressed as fine as any other lady; she was sponsored by a baroness, a marchioness, and a duchess. She had a smile and charm to put the town to shame, but neither could change the circumstances of her birth. She had been unfortunate enough to be sired by a mere country gentleman.

"Why the sigh, madam? A very longing sigh, it seemed. Would you rather be elsewhere?" the Duke asked breaking the awkward silence at last.

"I beg your pardon, your Grace," she answered demurely.

"I have never before seen you to be at a loss for words."

He had noticed. She could feel her colour rising and felt humiliated. *How dare he!*

"Please at least humour me and say something so I do not return home feeling as though it was my staid company at fault."

"I never would have thought you, of all people, would seek or appreciate flattery, your Grace." She almost snapped the words.

"And what, pray tell, do you base this assumption on?" he asked, lifting one haughty eyebrow.

2

"Your usual silence in my presence," she replied curtly.

"You injure me, Miss Craig." He brought her hand to his heart to feign injury and even proffered a slight, devastatingly handsome smile.

She was not fooled by his too-late attempt to be chivalrous.

"I intended no offence. Most of my thoughts are better left unsaid," he explained.

What Maili would not give to know them. She would be much more comfortable if he would speak and flirt as the other gentleman did. Instead, he always looked at her as though she bore a horn upon her head. She had no witty repartee for him and she hated it.

"Why do you think them better left unsaid? Are they improper?" she asked out of sheer curiosity.

He surprised her by twirling her away from the dance floor, down the terrace steps and to a pathway in the garden away from the revelries of the ball.

"Miss Craig," he began, then cleared his throat.

She waited patiently, though her pulse was racing and her breathing was causing her chest to rise and fall rapidly. She began to fumble with the green ribbon hanging from her gown. She looked up to see why he was quiet yet again, only to find him studying her with a dark, hungry look in his eyes.

Was he going to kiss her?

Voices grew closer along the path and he stepped away. She felt an unexpected sense of longing when she could no longer reach him.

"Lord and Lady Brennan." Cavenray greeted the couple coming towards them on the path with a bow. The lady smiled charmingly before dipping into a curtsy. Lord Brennan inclined his head.

"Will you do us the honour of introducing your companion, Cavenray? I have not had the pleasure," Lord Brennan asked.

"Certainly. Lord and Lady Brennan, may I present Miss Craig?"

Maili curtsied. The lady turned pale as though she had seen a ghost and grasped her husband with both hands. "Margaret?"

"No, my lady," Maili responded at once. "My mother was Margaret. Did you know her?"

"But you are dead!" Lady Brennan exclaimed, holding a hand over her mouth in obvious shock.

Maili was silent with disbelief. Did this stranger know her mother from long ago, and did she know of herself, Seamus and Catriona?

"Madam, I am quite alive, as are my brother and sister. My parents did perish, in a carriage accident well over a decade ago. Perhaps it is an uncanny coincidence?"

"No, you look exactly like Margaret Douglas, my sister by marriage."

"She was my mother." Maili whispered, instinctively fingering the locket around her neck which held the portrait of her mama.

The woman gasped again and shook her head in disbelief. "There must be some mistake. I do not understand how this could be. Where have you all been hidden, and why is your name Craig?"

Maili hesitated, trying to maintain her composure, though she was deeply confused. She was intrigued to know more, but did not wish to have this discussion in front of the Duke. It was no secret about her birth, but for some reason saying it aloud near him gave her pause, though he might be shocked to know she had any restraint. She lifted her chin and spoke anyway.

"After our parents' death, we were sent to Lord Vernon's orphanage in Scotland. There we befriended the gentleman who is now Lord Craig, and he became our guardian and gave us his name."

"But how did we not know? We were told you were dead," she repeated. "There was a funeral—you have graves in the family plot—and this entire time you have been in Scotland? And in an orphanage?"

"Not the entire time. We have been with the Craig family for many years now." In for a penny...

"Seamus married Lady Christelle Stanton in June, and Catriona married Lieutenant Holdsworth last summer. I am here with Lord and Lady Craig for the Season, though we shall be returning to Scotland tomorrow." She felt the Duke's arm stiffen beneath her hand. He must be sensitive to the reminder of his failed courtship with Lady Christelle.

"We have been in the country too long, Brennan," the lady said to her husband, who Maili could feel gazing at her. "To think I have missed your entire lives!" She began to fan herself as though she might swoon.

"And to think I have another family..." Maili whispered.

"Please do not overset yourself, Annie," Lord Brennan said dotingly. "Let us get you back to the house to rest and allow time for your nerves to settle. We have plenty of time to sort this out and become acquainted."

"Yes, of course. Would you call on me in the morning, Miss Craig? I would dearly love to spend a little time with you before we depart for the country. We were taking our leave just now so we could set off at first light, but you will not mind a slight delay, will you, Brennan?"

"Of course not, my dear. We would be delighted if you could, Miss Craig," Lord Brennan added kindly.

"I thank you. We were also to depart on the morrow, but I am certain my parents would not mind sparing me time to speak with you." Maili could scarcely believe the conversation she was having. She bit her lower lip to control the nervous laughter she felt threatening to pour out of her.

"Please come as soon as you like. We are country folk at heart and do not keep city hours, as you can see."

"I shall come after I break my fast, then. Good evening," Maili said as she curtsied and watched them depart, still trying to comprehend what had happened.

"Quite an unusual circumstance," the Duke said curtly, looking acutely uncomfortable as he shot his cuffs.

"Quite a potential scandal, you mean," she murmured.

He did not reply. Maili felt the inexplicable urge to cry, stunned by his indifference, even if he only knew her very little. How unfortunate that he, of all people, had borne witness to such an intimate moment!

"I think we should return to the ballroom. We have been gone some time," the Duke stated.

"Indeed." So many emotions roiled through her: disbelief, anger, happiness, hope... She did not know how it had happened, but she would try to be grateful for this chance with family she had never thought to have. And she tried to ignore the sensations of frustration she felt at the Duke's reaction, sensations it was difficult to put a name to.

~

Hugh Dickerson, Ninth Duke of Cavenray, sat alone in his study staring at the amber liquid in his glass, not really seeing it, lost in thought. In fact, he was wishing he had stayed at home at Sutton Hall this spring instead of coming to London. Having succumbed to the constant nagging of his dam and her desires for him to wed and secure the ducal line, he had reluctantly agreed to find a bride. Unfortunately, the Season had just drawn to a close with the Sefton ball this evening and he had no bride, nor yet prospects of one.

"Curse it all," he grumbled to himself, running his fingers through his black locks in frustration.

He had not wanted a bride, and now he had made a fool of himself by paying court to Lady Christelle—his mother's choice—and the lady had selected a country gentleman instead. His tender emotions were unaffected; perhaps his pride was to a minor extent, but he had not courted Lady Christelle in earnest because his heart had not been in it. A pair of fine grey eyes and lustrous red hair kept distracting him.

Hugh groaned and tipped back his glass and emptied it, relishing the warm glow it left as it travelled through him. For over a decade he had become expert at avoiding the marriage mart, including schemes to entrap him. And now, the only female to tempt him was ineligible. His mother had loudly pronounced he might as well marry a tavern wench when they had discussed the list of eligibles at the beginning of the Season. He cringed at the memory, but reluctantly had to agree. Miss Craig was not suited to be a duchess in the conventional sense— in any sense. Besides her merely genteel birth, the confounding woman never stopped talking or laughing; she did not know the meaning of decorum and she was simply...mesmerizing. He could not stop thinking about her or seeking her out or wanting her. He could not marry her; therefore, he must go as far away from her as humanly possible.

He could still hear his mother's diatribe echoing in his head because he had waltzed with the girl tonight.

"Offer her a slip on the shoulder, if you must, after you are married, but for heaven's sake do not court her in society!" She had dressed him down as though he were still in leading strings.

"You go too far, Mother," he had reprimanded in a calm, quiet voice that was an ominous sound to anyone who knew him well. He had allowed her to influence him by remaining silent on the matter. He permitted his mother a great deal of licence, but he no longer needed nor sought her opinion. Look at where it had landed him.

Hugh wrinkled his face with disgust. He abhorred conflict and he knew he had offended the Duchess, but he did not want a society marriage with mistresses and affairs—like his parents'. He should encourage his brothers to wed and secure the Dukedom. No woman would want him for anything other than the title. Perhaps that had been the appeal of Miss Craig. She had been the one person to treat him as though he were simply a man. Her obvious disregard for his opinion was so very appealing.

He set his glass down on the side table with a clink. He was finished playing the puppet to his mother's every whim. Only a fool would agree to such madness, and he could not say why he had. But he was finished.

Hugh had allowed the ducal mask to fall and come very close to making a fatal mistake tonight. Dancing with Miss Craig was the first thing he had done because he had wanted to during the entirety of his time in Town. A few moments more, and he would have been caught in a compromising position in the Seftons' garden. Well, he hoped she would have allowed a kiss, though she might have planted him a facer. He chuckled. The poor innocent did not seem to have any idea of his attraction to her, nor her inherent charms... Yet a lifetime as his Duchess...would ruin her spirit. She would hate him.

What a strange turn of events the evening had taken. Lady Brennan had nearly swooned when she had seen Miss Craig, thinking she was her dead sister or some such oddity. Then the interlude with Miss Craig had come to an abrupt halt as he had not known what to say to the poor girl when she had needed comfort. He had almost pulled her into his arms.

Hugh sighed. He would be forced into many such females' company for the next fortnight. Why had he agreed to a house party? He very likely had not. Two weeks with his mother nagging and young misses being paraded before him... no, he was quite sure he had not willingly consented to such a scheme. Perhaps it was time for a visit to one of the other estates. Yes. He was a duke, by Jove, and he was not obligated to attend a house party, marry, or make a fool of himself by pining after anyone in public. If he could be alone for a while, he was certain he could manage his animal urges and find reason again.

CHAPTER 2

*M*aili had made her excuses to her remaining partners and asked to be taken home straight away. She had been too overcome to tell Margaux and Gavin what had happened and had gone to bed as soon as she arrived home at Craig House.

However, she found she could not sleep due to the excitement of finding some of her father's family, and also from considering what it might mean. Perhaps there would be no scandal and there was a simple explanation. She did not wish to think anyone could have knowingly sent Seamus, Catriona and her to an orphanage and disguised their parents' deaths. Had it been some awful mistake? She had been young, but she still remembered how it had felt to be abandoned in a strange place and missing her parents. Many children were not so fortunate as they had been—they'd had a good life and were loved by Gavin and Margaux. She wiped away the tears that had begun to form at the memories.

Reluctantly, she gave up on anymore sleep and rang for the maid. She pulled on a day dress of jonquil muslin, lost in thought as the maid tied her laces. She did not know what to make of it all, though she was very much inclined to like her aunt and wanted to know her better. She was the youngest and therefore had known her parents the least. If only they had more time, she thought sadly, as she noticed the packed trunks in her room.

She would need to tell Gavin and Margaux the whole, but how would they react? Would they hinder her contact with them? They could not really forbid it since she was of age, but she did not want to hurt them by getting to know her family. However, the curiosity was almost overwhelming. Catriona had told her over and over what she remembered of their parents, but it was never enough.

Maili looked at herself in the glass and then at the miniature locket she had of her mother. Perhaps she did resemble her. The woman in the portrait was so very beautiful and elegant. Maili did not feel beautiful or elegant. After the events of the Season, despite the court of gentlemen who had followed her and Christelle, she did not harbour any flattering delusions. Courting her had all been about amusement. Any serious thoughts had been directed to Christelle's quarter. The gentlemen might enjoy her company, but as they would that of a little sister or one of their school friends.

And the Duke; she had to stop herself from grinding her teeth. The Duke made her feel small and insignificant and she loathed him for it. He was handsome and powerful and his bearing reminded everyone else that they were not. That hooded disapproving gaze of his, and his languid grace that was second nature to him, were constant reminders of her own inferiority.

She pinned the last curl up and stood. It was time to leave London behind and the pompous Duke with it. She headed for the breakfast parlour to speak to her parents. Would they understand?

"Good morning, Mama, Papa." She greeted each with a kiss on the cheek.

"Maili, you are about early after a ball," Gavin remarked.

"I could not sleep well," Maili replied as she began to fill her plate from the sideboard.

"Did something happen at the ball?" Margaux asked with concern.

"I suppose so," she replied as she placed some kippers and toast on her plate before turning back to the table.

Both Gavin and Margaux were staring at her, clearly waiting for her to elaborate.

"I met my father's sister, Lady Brennan."

She looked up cautiously to see if they understood. Their faces held the shock she had felt the night before.

"But how?" Margaux asked.

"I was walking in the garden with the Duke of Cavenray, and we happened upon Lord and Lady Brennan. Lady Brennan took quite a fright at the sight of me and mistook me for my mother, Margaret."

"But you had no family left. That is why you were at the Alberfoyle orphanage," Margaux said, looking confused.

"Yes, that is what we believed, and Lady Brennan also thought we were dead. At least that is what she was told. She said we have head-stones in the family plot at Crossings."

Gavin was very quiet and his normally jovial demeanour disappeared.

"What do you make of it, Papa?" Maili asked.

"I think someone has much to answer for, but that is not for you to worry over."

"What do you mean to do?"

"I will begin by checking the records at Alberfoyle. Every child has a file with the details of their entry into the orphanage, which is very useful for situations such as this," he said calmly.

"That is a good idea," Margaux agreed.

"We need to tell Seamus and Catriona," Maili said.

"Yes, you may write to Seamus after we have stopped and checked the records at the orphanage. Catriona can be told when we arrive home."

Maili hesitated. "My, my...Lady Brennan has asked me to go and visit her this morning."

"Pardon?" Gavin said at the same time as Margaux. "Surely you cannot think to..."

"I, I think I would like to go." She swallowed nervously. "I know so little about my parents that I would like the chance to know more."

"I see," Gavin said, and Maili wondered if she had hurt his feelings.

Could they understand it did not lessen her love or appreciation for them? She needed to explore this link to her parents.

"Someone had to have knowingly deceived if you have headstones. What if they did not wish you found, and if knowing you are alive threatens them in some way?" Gavin went on as her thoughts strayed.

"That is a chance I am willing to take. The lady seemed genuinely surprised and delighted to have found me."

"I suppose there is little harm in a tête-à-tête this morning while the carriages are packed," Gavin said.

"I will go with you. I would like an introduction," Margaux said, with a wary look at Gavin.

"Thank you, Mama and Papa!" Maili smiled with the excitement she felt, and hurried from the room to fetch her bonnet.

Margaux and Maili pulled up before Lord and Lady Brennan's town house. The garden joined with that of Lady Sefton's and now Maili understood why, the night before, Lord and Lady Brennan had said they were taking their leave through the garden.

"I am so pleased you came!" Lady Brennan greeted them in the entrance hall, amongst the bustle of packing, before the butler could escort them to the drawing room. The normally elegant hall was piled high with trunks and Maili could see much of the house had already been shrouded in Holland covers, much like their own town home.

"Lady Brennan, may I present my mother, Margaux, Lady Craig. Mama, this is my aunt, Lady Brennan."

The two women curtsied and eyed the other discreetly. Lady Brennan was pretty in the light-haired, light-eyed, conventionally English way, and her mama was striking in a dark, exotic way.

"You are just as beautiful as they say. I believe we missed each other by a few seasons," Lady Brennan said kindly.

"You are too kind. I am very *enceinte*. Thankfully, my mother enjoys gallivanting about and did not mind chaperoning Maili for me. My two sisters are also with child."

"Please come and sit down. This room has not yet been fully covered." Lady Brennan led them into the drawing room, to two gold brocaded sofas. "We rarely come to town. Brennan is eager to return to the country, but I am so happy we came this year. He would not have been persuaded if it had not been for a Bill he wished to vote on."

"Yes, it is much the same with us. We prefer the country but Maili has always wished for a Season," Margaux answered, seeming to be at ease with the situation.

"This must be as much of a shock to you as it has been to us. I cannot say how thankful I am that you and Lord Craig brought up her and the others as your own. Anyone can see how fortunate she is."

"I thank you. We do love her as our own," Margaux agreed with a tender touch to Maili's arm.

"I am also grateful for the opportunity to know her a little better. I feel as though I have been robbed of time. I know that to say such a thing may seem melodramatic, but I feel vapourish to know the children were abandoned to an orphanage!" she remarked with obvious disgust.

"At least we have found each other now," Maili said gently.

"It brings me to my proposition. I know it is sudden, and I understand if you are uncomfortable with the notion, but I would like to invite you to join us at Brantley. All of you."

Maili sucked in her breath, but knew she should not blurt out her acceptance as she wished to.

"There are many questions I would like answered before I could think to agree to such a visit," Margaux said candidly.

Maili tensed. She hoped her mama would not offend Lady Brennan.

"I do understand. It is such a bizarre turn of events."

"Were the children thought to have been killed in the same accident as their parents?"

"Yes, of course." Lady Brennan looked affronted and confused.

"Did anyone look for them?"

"I- I assume so. I never thought they needed looking for—when I saw their graves—" She had to stop and compose herself. She was visibly upset. Maili had the same questions, but Margaux was almost accusatory in her queries.

"Mama, it is clear my aunt truly believed us dead."

"Yes, please forgive me. I would just like to know who is responsible for such an act."

"Perhaps my brother, David, knows more, but he has been abroad since the accident."

"Abroad?" Margaux asked, her voice laced with doubt or surprise. Maili could not be sure which.

"Yes. So you see, I have had no other family for the past ten years other than my sons, and I would dearly love to know Maili better. I will have Lord Brennan write to David and see what may be discovered."

"Unfortunately, we need to return to Scotland. I know Catriona and John are very capable, but we have been absent a long time and my husband will wish me to be at home for my confinement."

"Oh, yes, of course! I am certain you are as anxious as we are to see home," she replied, evidently trying to hide her disappointment.

"Mama, may I not go alone?" Maili suggested.

"I could not make that decision without your father," Margaux answered.

"Perhaps we could drive over as we leave Town and collect her if he consents, and be on our way if not?" Lady Brennan offered.

Margaux nodded. "We are also ready to depart. That seems a sensible idea."

"I am very grateful to you for considering this, Lady Craig. Somehow, it makes me feel closer to my brother Nigel to know he still exists through them."

Lady Brennan showed them to their carriage and agreed to call in two hours' time.

"I cannot like you being there alone with no one to turn to should you find trouble," Lord Craig said when the ladies had returned home and apprised him of the offer. "I know very little about Lord and Lady Brennan or Sir David Douglas."

"Where is their estate? Lady Brennan did not mention it," Margaux said.

"Westmorland, I believe. I looked in *The Peerage*," Maili replied, trying to recall precisely what she had read.

Margaux and Gavin exchanged looks.

"It could be worse, I suppose. It would not take too long for you to reach home by stage or post with a maid if absolutely necessary," he said resignedly.

"You may leave me precise instructions and funds if need be. I assure you, I will be able to manage," Maili said confidently.

"It is not you we worry about, my dear."

"But may I go?"

"She seemed genuine, Gavin," Margaux confessed.

"You will write to me and keep me informed. I will send you a letter when we reach Alberfoyle—or we will come to fetch you post-haste if I am not satisfied. I believe your uncle has much to answer for, but since he is abroad and Margaux is comfortable with Lady Brennan, I will allow a short visit."

"Oh, thank you, Papa and Mama!" she said, making no effort to hide her open glee.

Gavin looked heavenward. "I still doona like it, lass."

He must go to the ends of the earth, Cavenray decided. It was the only way. He had estates in Cornwall, Westmorland, Kent and Scotland and his seat in East Anglia, which was where the house party was to be held. Cornwall was the farthest, but it could be devilish hot there at this time of year, and if he recalled correctly, there was a new roof being fitted. That would be most unpleasant to endure while on holiday. Westmorland would have to do, since he was not quite desperate enough to go abroad, and the Lakes were lovely in the summer. Hopefully the entirety of England would not also think so.

He called for Martin, his secretary.

"Yes, your Grace?" the secretary enquired upon entering.

"I will be leaving on the morrow for Gracemere. Please send word to the steward to make the necessary arrangements. I shall require you to deliver a letter for the Duchess, informing her of my decision but omitting my choice of refuge."

"Of course, sir." His secretary masked any surprise he must have felt at this announcement.

"Her Grace may matchmake for my brothers with my blessing," Hugh explained.

He smiled at the thought. Having endured enough barbs at his brothers' instigation, he felt not the least remorse for leaving them to the mercy of his mother's machinations. They were old enough to fend off the intent misses and mamas. There was no shame in marrying into the Cavenray clan and bearing its heirs.

"Your Grace?"

"Yes, Martin?"

"The Duchess sent over a final guest list for your perusal and wanted to know if you had any last-minute additions."

Hugh clenched his jaw and only just refrained from spewing the string of foul words which came to mind. He would swear the woman could read his thoughts and knew he was wavering.

"Tell her I have no care for who she invites— in that polite way you phrase things, of course." He waved his hand as he spoke.

"Very good, sir."

"And Martin, do not deliver my note to her on the morrow until I am several counties away."

"Naturally, your Grace," his secretary replied with a twinkle in his eye.

Martin deserved higher wages, Hugh decided, and made a mental note to see to it.

He relaxed and let out a sigh of relief, having made the decision to take control of this part of his life. He would not be bullied into marrying for dynastic alliances. The Cavenray dynasty was quite impressive on its own. He sat down to pen the missive to his mother. He was feeling quite proud of his decision and therefore was freer of hand and pithiness than was his custom with her.

To Her Grace the Duchess of Cavenray,

By the time this reaches you, I will be far away from Cambridge. Forgive my informing you by note, but I am not to be persuaded. I have decided against marrying. There is no reason why one of my illustrious brothers may not marry and carry on the line. I wish you joy in matchmaking on their behalf, and a successful house party.

P.S. Send word to Marvin when the happy event is to take place and I will return from ~~seclusion~~, my sojourn.

Your obedient servant,
Cavenray

Hugh realized everyone would think him to be nursing a broken heart over Lady Christelle, but it could not be helped. He must remove himself from anything and everything likely to remind him of marriage and Maili Craig.

He folded the letter, sealed it with sense of relief and placed it on the desk for Martin to deliver in the morning. He walked to his chamber and went to bed with a new-found peace of mind.

CHAPTER 3

*H*ugh rose before dawn, which was quite early on a summer's day, and donned his riding attire. He ran down the stairs with a spring in his step, eager to be on his way to Gracemere. Had he been of a nature to chuckle, he might even have done so at that moment—such was his relief.

He entered the breakfast room and was filling his plate high, so that later on, he would not be obligated to stop sooner than necessary for hunger, when he heard a throat clear. That was a sound he had not expected. Nevertheless, he did not turn to face her immediately.

"Good morning, your Grace. You are awake early." Early being an understatement. To his knowledge, she never descended from her apartments before noon, and yet now she had come to his town house at this hour of the morning?

"I did not care for the tone in your note," she said curtly.

Which note? Had Martin already delivered the second epistle? Surely not...

"It is true. I care not whom you invite." He would not incriminate himself unnecessarily.

She eyed him suspiciously. It was the look which made him feel as if he should still be wearing short coats. He would not be intimidated, though he ought to tell her in person of his true intentions... but he knew better.

"You look like you are dressed for riding. Are you leaving for Cambridge this morning?"

He did not wish to lie, but again, he was too old for the constant interrogation. It was why he still had a separate abode in town, though Cavenray House was large enough for a small army.

"Shall I fill a plate for you?" he asked lazily, putting off the question as before and placing his own plate on the table.

She shook her head. "I do not eat at this ungodly hour."

He waved a hand to intimate 'as you wish', before answering her earlier question.

"I have business to attend to. When do you leave town?"

"Today. It is why I am here so early. I hoped to catch you and make certain you were not going to cry off."

Suddenly his food lodged in his throat and he had to cough to keep from choking. He took a drink while he thought how to answer.

"Forgive me. What would it matter if I did cry off? The ladies can certainly make excellent matches in Ashley and Stephen."

"You promised me, Hugh." Her voice had changed to a familiar whine; it was guaranteed to make him cringe and give in as quickly as possible. He could never abide female dramatics.

"I promised to look for a wife this Season, your Grace. I courted your choice; she declined the offer. I upheld my end of the bargain. Even if I attend your house party, I will not promise to marry." He infused his voice with a finality he rarely used towards his mother. He loathed having to speak to her this way in order to make her understand.

She stared at him long and hard, and he met her gaze with the most complacent look he could manage. She had to understand he would not waver.

Instead of delivering the tirade he had grown accustomed to receiving from her, she stood up.

"Very well. If that is your decision. I will hope you change your mind. No marriage is better than marriage to someone like the Craig chit," she added with uncharacteristic resignation.

It took a great deal of effort to keep his face impassive and his tongue still by clenching his jaw. He was certain his eyes flashed with anger, if she had but been looking.

How could he fault her when he had come to the same decision? But it was not her decision, and in any case, was that not why he was leaving?

"Good day, your Grace."

"Mother. I am your mother. You only say 'your Grace' to me in private when you are angry with me. Did you realize that?"

It was a direct hit, straight through his heart.

"I wish it had not come to this, Mother. I came to realize this past spring, however, that I can fulfil my duties to my title without being miserable—I hope."

"You would not have been miserable with Lady Christelle," she protested.

"Perhaps not, but she would have been. She deserves better than I can give her. I cannot abide a marriage with no affection, no loyalty." He held up his hand before she could object. "Please do not bother to protest. My decision is final. I wish you joy of matchmaking with my brothers. Give them my regards."

She sighed in frustration but held her thoughts within. She inclined her head and started out of the door before stopping and looking over her shoulder. "I want only what is best for you. If you come to your senses..."

He shook his head and her eyes fell in disappointment before she turned and left.

Was it too early for a drink? Hugh looked upward for answers and gained no reply. That had been painful, but it was best to have told her in person.

With that task over with and breakfast no longer appealing, he called for his gloves, coat and crop before he went to burn the letter that would be moot.

Now that he was mounted and finally on his way, he was going to leave London and the disastrous events of the Season behind him. As soon as he had passed through the Tottenham toll-gate, he inhaled as deeply as he could of the fresh country air while riding and felt invigorated—almost as if he was starting afresh.

He laughed and patted his stallion's black neck. Nothing, absolutely nothing, was pressing for his attention the whole summer. He would take long walks, go fishing, have a nap in the sun if he wished— essentially nothing ducal. He could not remember feeling this giddy since he was a small boy in fact; perhaps that was the last time he had been to Gracemere. It had been too long. Perhaps that was also why he rarely went, since it held such memories of his father.

~

Maili tried to contain her excitement so she did not appear as vulgar as the Duke thought her, but she loved adventure and this was a great one. They had settled in the smart travelling carriage led by a team of four well-matched chestnuts, and were supplied with a hamper of fruits, fresh bread, cheeses and wine. There were also books and natting for her pleasure, if she desired.

"Where do we begin, dear Maili? I want to know everything, but perhaps I should tell you what you have to look forward to, first," her aunt said as she settled herself on the rose-coloured velvet seats.

"Oh, yes please." Maili held her hands still instead of clapping them as she wished to do.

"We have a lovely estate, if I do say so myself. It borders one of the famous lakes you hear tell of by the poets and extends over to the mountains and sea. If you enjoy painting, this area is a favourite of many artists."

"It sounds a dream come true."

"To me, it is. 'Tis why my Brennan and I never leave! And very likely why you and I are only now discovering each other," she said with a sad look.

"We cannot change the past, Aunt."

Her aunt looked at her with a warm smile. "If only everyone could have such a sunny nature. We have three boys and they are all away at school. It seems much lonelier with them gone and I now live for the holidays, although I confess I also relish the peace and quiet at times," she said with a guilty grin.

"I do understand. Will I be able to meet them? I, too, want to know everything! I will try to ration questions so as to not wear out my welcome before we arrive." Maili laughed.

"I do not think it is possible, child. After being used to three boys at once I think you should be quite manageable, and besides, I have longed for a girl to fuss over. I hope you do not mind. Please tell me if I become overbearing."

"I do not think it possible. Have you met Lady Ashbury?" Maili asked with a playful look.

"Indeed, I have," Lady Brennan acknowledged with a smile. "Now begin your story with what you remember, and perhaps by the time we arrive we will have reached the present."

"Where shall we start?" Maili asked.

"Your uncle told me quite a bit about you last night."

"My uncle Brennan?"

"Yes, of course. I have not communicated with David yet."

Maili longed to ask more about David but she dared not yet. She needed to grow more comfortable first.

"So, my uncle Brennan knew of me?"

"Through talk at his clubs," she agreed. "He did not realize you were my niece, of course. He says that you have had many suitors and a court of notable gentleman surrounding you the entire Season."

Maili could feel her cheeks heating. She had heard of the gentlemen's clubs, and the betting books and what some of the discussions entailed, from her brother and overheard gossip too. It was usually unflattering to the ladies involved.

"Do not worry. He did not hear anything unsavoury," Lady Brennan remarked, her gaze on Maili's face.

Nothing he would repeat to you, Maili thought to herself.

"Did nothing come of any of the suitors?" her aunt asked.

"There were some offers," Maili admitted.

"There were none Lord Craig approved of?"

"There were none that I approved of," she confessed quietly, realizing she sounded spoiled.

Her aunt raised her eyebrows in either disapproval or surprise. Maili was not sure which. "What are you waiting for? What do you seek in a suitor?"

Maili sighed loudly. "I am not certain. It is likely to be my only Season." She shook her head to fight off the sudden wetness filling her eyes at the knowledge.

Her aunt eyed her sympathetically. "Is your heart already spoken for?"

What a ridiculous notion! "No, it was quite different from my expectations. I suppose I had always dreamed of a Cinderella story, where the orphan finds her prince. Instead, if you will forgive my plain speaking, I found pompous dukes and men offering me a slip on the shoulder."

Lady Brennan gasped in obvious offence and threw her hand against her chest. "How dare they!"

"Indeed. Apparently, I was a great gun to them, but my birth was considered too low for most of the gentlemen. It would seem my uncle neglected to mention that Lady Christelle was always with me. The gentlemen surrounding us were looking for her hand, not courting me."

Lady Brennan looked her in the eye. "I think you underestimate yourself. I imagine you must believe such sentiments, since you came out with a duke's daughter. She created quite a sensation with her story. Even I knew of it."

"And she and Seamus made a love match."

Lady Brennan smiled. "It makes my heart happy to know it. But now you, my dear, must not sell yourself short. Your birth is not as low as you seem to think it is. Your conviction is understandable, considering you knew little about your family."

"We knew little more than he was a country gentleman."

"Ah," her aunt said with understanding. "Your grandfather, my father, was a baronet. Your papa Douglas would be Sir Nigel, had

23

he lived."

"It is still not lofty enough for a duke," she muttered.

Lady Brennan pretended not to hear and continued, "Your father never cared for Society or titles. He only wanted to be a gentleman farmer."

Maili looked up, hanging on every word about her parents.

Her aunt stared off into the distance as though lost in a long-ago memory. "Margaret and I were the best of friends and your father fell in love with her. She turned down many offers in order to have him— even a duke and an earl. She was very like you."

"I had no such offers, aunt."

"What of the man you were with last evening?" her aunt asked, her eyes searching hopefully.

"Do not put your hope in that quarter, I beg you. Cavenray has no designs on me!"

"Ah, I thought...but never you mind. The current Duchess was not always kind to poor Margaret. She was incredibly jealous of her—not that she held any blame. It was quite common knowledge that the Duke and Duchess' marriage was loveless. Fortunately, your mother was oblivious to anyone but dear Nigel."

"And my mother's birth?"

"Better than mine," her aunt answered. "She was the only child of an Irish earl."

Maili sat quietly for some time, pondering the new information about her parents. She scoffed to herself about not being good enough for the Duke. Would the Duke and Duchess look down their lofty noses at her now?

CHAPTER 4

"Two days?" Hugh asked in disbelief, trying not to use the ducal voice.

"Yessir," the ostler replied. "They do not work on the Lord's Day, and the smithy is already closed for today."

Not even thirty miles from London and Goliath had thrown a shoe. Hugh was determined to be an ordinary gentleman on this trip. He had sent his valet, Emory, who also acted as majordomo, ahead, and his secretary had remained in London. He did not wish to proclaim his title to receive any advantage. Why was he in such a hurry, after all? He was free—for a little while, anyway.

"Thank you. Can you recommend an inn?" Emory was to have procured a room for him further along the route, but he was stopping short of his intended goal for the day.

"The Cat and Owl has decent fare and might have a room. Their ale is the best around."

Making arrangements for Goliath to remain at the livery stable, Hugh tipped his hat and pulled his saddlebag onto his shoulder before walking towards the small, shabby inn that looked like it needed a new roof. He said a silent prayer that the rains would hold off until his horse's shoe was repaired.

It rained cats and dogs for the entire two days. Perhaps even an owl or two. He thought he could hear one from time to time when the din of the taproom finally quietened down in the wee, small hours before dawn.

He crawled from his damp straw mattress with an aching back, sneezing and determined to fight the threatening chill. He would not stay another day in this inn. He ordered and ate a meat pie with ale and swung his bag over his back again, determined to bribe the smith with whatever was necessary to have the shoe repaired that day.

Fortunately, the smith was finishing shoeing Goliath as he walked in.

Having paid the man, he mounted the stallion and they were soon trudging through the mud at a turtle's pace. He had hoped to be past halfway to Gracemere by this time. At this rate, summer would be over before he arrived. He at last reached the inn his valet had originally procured for him as the sun was beginning to set.

His mood was grey when he set out on the fourth day of his journey. He rarely travelled this road and was unfamiliar with the posting houses. At least he had been able to keep his own horse due to the slow pace. The rains had let up, but the roads were still a mud-bath. Part of him wished he had stayed in London and succumbed to the temptation of one fiery redhead. He loved a challenge and she would be the greatest one of his life. But there was only disaster ahead in that direction so he forged onward to Gracemere, one slow step at a time.

When he was at his last stop on the journey, less than one day away from his estate, he was coming down the steps to dine when he heard a familiar voice. He halted in place instead of advancing into the taproom. A chill and flashes of memory swept over him from his days at Eton and Cambridge. He had not seen Deuce since then and had heard little of him. Hugh was hesitant to make himself known. It was ridiculous that an older bully could still provoke feelings of rancour, he thought, reflectively rubbing the scar on his chin he had received courtesy of the man who had received the nickname of Deuce for revealing his double-sided self. The day Deuce had been expelled from Cambridge, when his gambling ring had been exposed, had come as an inordinate relief.

The voice grew lower and Hugh began to wonder if he had imagined it. He put his head down and went through the smoky room to a table in the back corner, hoping to be discreet. While he certainly did not have his usual crisp, tidy look without his valet's machinations, he was unmistakably a gentleman and would be observed and perhaps recognized if Deuce bothered to look up.

When he passed by the table, the group of men seated at it was huddled close together. Paying them no mind, he walked on and sat down on a high-backed settle in a dark corner, signalling for service. Once the serving maid brought his food, he concentrated on his stew and ale, sneaking covert glances without lifting his gaze from his plate.

There were four men, and Hugh was hard-pressed to make out which one was Deuce. All looked rough, weathered, and like men you would steer your womenfolk across the street to avoid. The dull rumble of voices in the room kept him from overhearing anything they discussed, but from their secretive manner, Hugh surmised it was something unpleasant.

He wondered what Deuce could have been up to all these years. The man had come from a well-respected family, but Hugh had not even heard of him since the day of the old Duke's death. Clearly, he had absented himself from polite society, and Hugh could not think he would want to renew their old acquaintance. Could the man have fallen on such hard times he was reduced to fishing? This village was near the sea, and it was how most of the occupants earned their daily bread. He sat there, pondering how different life was now from how he had thought it would be when he had been a fresh buck on the town, just up from Cambridge.

The men pushed back from the table, as if agreeing on something, then took their leave. Subconsciously, Hugh studied them and when Deuce turned, he saw the familiar grey eyes flash the menacing look he'd had at university, only it appeared much more cynical and sinister. He wore a thick beard and a common labourer's clothing that appeared none too clean. The hair on Hugh's neck stood up in warning, and he forced himself to avert his eyes before they made contact. He hoped it was the last he would see of Deuce.

~

Finally, after a week of travelling in the carriage, they made it to Brantley. The estate was truly picturesque as they traversed through the hilly woodlands and deer park before arriving at the house, which was set off by a parterre garden in front of it. The neoclassical mansion was situated to look out over the surrounding hills, lake and Irish Sea.

They had barely arrived before several days of rain kept them indoors. Maili had spent so much time with her aunt Brennan that she felt very comfortable. She was pleased to find the lady most amiably disposed. It was easy to see why her mother had loved her as a dear friend. She had light hair and the grey eyes of the Douglas family and was still very handsome.

Maili had tried to draw out as much information as possible about her uncle David, but Lady Brennan seemed reluctant to speak of him. He had lived abroad for many years, and he was reclusive—that was all she was able to ascertain about his current status.

She did discover the uncle had inherited a very tidy estate from her father's death—one which should have belonged to Seamus. Maili did not want to think poorly of an uncle she could not remember, but how could he not have been informed they were still alive? Something did not feel right. She realized she did not even know the name of the village they had lived in before her parents' death. She would have to ask.

If her uncle Douglas had known they were alive and sent them to the orphanage, it was not really a crime. It was in very poor taste. Stealing an inheritance from Seamus, however, was another matter. She would refrain from passing judgement until more information was known, but she would try to gather knowledge while she was here.

Before the first week came to a close, the rain eased and they were able to visit the vicarage for tea. Mrs. Snodgrass was a pleasant and plump matron. Maili liked her instantly.

"Oh, Lady Brennan! You did not tell me you had a guest," the woman said, appearing surprised when she saw Maili.

"It was unexpected—pleasantly so. This is my niece, whom I thought long dead, Geraldine. May I present Maili Douglas...Craig." They both made their curtsies.

"I am pleased to make your acquaintance, madam," Maili said politely.

"And I am pleased to make yours. Do come in! Tea is ready, and you can explain while we enjoy one of God's greatest delights over a comfortable cose." The matron indicated some well-worn but inviting sofas for them to sit upon.

"Now, this is one of Sir Nigel's daughters?" Mrs. Snodgrass asked while taking her full measure.

"Indeed, she is. I still cannot believe our good fortune in finding one another. We happened upon each other in a garden and I thought she was Margaret!" Lady Brennan explained.

"She is the spitting image of her, I'll agree," Mrs. Snodgrass remarked, taking a bite of a scone oozing with jam.

"You knew my mother as well?" Maili asked in surprise.

"Of course, I did. They lived but one parish away on the north side of the lake. They were forever visiting your aunt and uncle here-abouts," Mrs. Snodgrass explained while she served them more warm, buttered scones and tea. "I remember you as a wee babe."

"So, we lived nearby?"

"Aye, no more than ten miles away," Mrs. Snodgrass replied.

"Do you think we could see it while I am visiting?" Maili asked her aunt.

Her aunt Brennan hesitated but she hid it quickly. "I am sure something can be arranged."

"Where have you been all these years?" the matron enquired.

"We were taken to an orphanage after my parents died and were adopted by Lord and Lady Craig a few years later."

29

"So that is where the name Craig came from. I did not think you were married."

"No, I am afraid not."

"Did no one strike your fancy in London?" the woman asked boldly, without any apparent awareness of it.

"There were many amiable gentlemen, but none I would choose for marriage," Maili explained.

"I see," Mrs. Snodgrass said with a twinkle in her eye, while glancing at Lady Brennan. "Mayhap a country gentleman would be more your style. While I am not one for gossiping, word has it that Gracemere has family in residence for the first time in nigh-on fifteen years."

Maili looked up to determine the significance of this remark from her aunt's reaction; she was shaking her head at Mrs. Snodgrass. What was afoot?

"What is Gracemere?" Maili asked.

"It is the summer cottage of a duke. I am certain he does not wish to be known. He scarcely visits," Lady Brennan answered.

A mystery, Maili thought. However, her current opinion of dukes was that they could keep to themselves with her good riddance.

"How long do you intend to bless us with your presence?" the vicar's wife asked.

"I hope to stay for the remainder of the summer, or until my aunt tires of me. Lady Craig will be near her confinement soon afterwards and I would wish to be there for the event."

"Of course, you would, my dear." Lady Brennan agreed.

"Well, then, we had best arrange some good-natured fun while you are here, so we may leave a worthy impression of Westmorland."

"Oh, that will not be necessary, Mrs. Snodgrass, though it is very kind of you. After the whirl of London, I am very happy to hang up my dancing slippers for a while."

"Oh, pish! A beautiful young girl like you? I do not believe a word of it!"

Maili was *almost* speechless. "I assure you, madam, I am in earnest."

"Very well, then, I will give you a week. Then you will be begging me for entertainment," Mrs. Snodgrass agreed with self-satisfaction etched on her face.

Maili looked at her aunt, who was smiling fondly at the vicar's wife. Why was she not saying anything? She seemed quite distracted.

Mrs. Snodgrass was still talking. "We certainly have a few eligible men we can arrange for the assembly room, do we not, Annie?"

Maili wanted to groan aloud and run back to Brantley, then lock herself in her room for a fortnight. She wanted nothing to do with any gentlemen for a long while.

"Has anything happened since we were away?" Lady Brennan asked Mrs. Snodgrass.

"As a matter of fact, several things," she answered with an infectious grin. "Sally Hinton had twins again, the poor dear, and old man Spivey went to meet his maker."

"The poor old dear," Lady Brennan echoed.

"I am sorry if this bores you, Miss Craig. It will not offend me if you want to take a turn about the garden. I remember my mother would drone on and on for hours with her friends until I thought I would perish." The matron gave her a wink.

Maili smiled. "I do love talking, but I confess I know not a soul of whom you speak."

"We will remedy that soon enough," she replied.

Maili stood and walked to the window. There was an inviting flower garden behind the vicarage.

"Tell me, is there anything else?" her aunt asked.

"Well, there are rumours that the *gentleman gang* have started up again," Mrs. Snodgrass confided in a loud whisper.

"Oh?"

The woman nodded with a satisfied murmur at being the first to provide the information to Lady Brennan.

"Recently, the menfolk have had a lot more work and there seems to be funds available, if you know what I mean."

"I suppose that is a blessing," Lady Brennan replied, sounding unsure. "I wonder what made them start up again?"

"I do not know, but there was a big wreck off the coast, and the

Revenue men have been swarming all over the place, asking questions. They believe it was done intentionally."

Lady Brennan gasped.

Maili's interest was piqued. She thought smuggling was something related to pirates and the novels of Mrs. Radcliffe!

"Who is leading them now?" her aunt asked very quietly, and Maili had to strain to hear.

"It has all been kept secret. I have not heard a whisper of who it could be this time."

The ladies moved back to discussing villagers Maili did not know, much to her disappointment, so she ventured out into the garden. It was in full bloom—the lilies and peonies in bright colour and their fragrance sweet. She sat on the rope swing and allowed her feet to dangle while she swayed. She had enjoyed London, but the country was home to her. She tilted her face to the sun and thought about how much she had wanted to go to London. Catriona had been correct about many things – Maili certainly was not sophisticated enough, but her birth was better than she had imagined. Interestingly enough, she felt no different.

She did not know what would be left for her at home since she had not found a husband. It was not something she had allowed herself to contemplate.

CHAPTER 5

*H*ugh's mood was rather black by the time he finally rode through the gates of Gracemere. It had taken five more days for him to arrive than it should have. No matter, he was here now, and he felt his tension easing as bitter-sweet memories engulfed him. He had last taken this path the summer his father died. It had been their final time together.

He walked Goliath slowly along the arched avenue lining the drive from the gate, past the gardens and around to the stables. He dismounted and looked out over the sea, feeling the wind whip at him. This was precisely what he needed.

"Your Grace!" an elderly retainer exclaimed as he came rushing out to greet him.

"Watson."

"We were not sure when you would arrive, seeing as you did not turn up when expected. We were growing worried."

"I imagine Emory was beside himself. I was caught in the rains and mud from almost London onwards."

"May I say, we are delighted to have you at Gracemere once again, your Grace?" the butler said with undisguised delight.

"Believe me, Watson, I am just as happy to be here. It has been too long. I need a holiday from society," he replied amiably.

"We kept the small staff, as your man instructed."

"Yes, the quieter the better for me. I do not intend to entertain."

"Of course, your Grace. Shall I have tea prepared or a bath readied?"

"A bath followed by tea would be very welcome."

"Very good, your Grace." The man bowed and hurried away to impart instructions.

Days in the saddle had left Hugh stiff and sore. A nice long soak was just what was in order. By the time he entered his apartments, Emory was pouring some peppermint oil into his steaming bath.

"It seems I came ahead of the rain and you did not. You are a sight for sore eyes, your Grace, if I may say so," his valet said with unusual geniality.

"You may. I am pleased to see you, as well, and I appreciate your refraining from remarking on my appearance." Hugh had not shaved and his Hessians had not been properly polished since he had left London. Emory seemed so happy to see him that he was being uncommonly gracious about it all.

"What have you been doing with your time, Emory?" Hugh asked with rare curiosity as he began to remove his waistcoat and shirt.

"Awaiting your arrival, of course," the valet remarked, the implication being, as if he would be doing anything else.

One brow raised, Hugh cast him a questioning glance.

"Well, I might have taken a turn around the village."

"And? Is it safe?"

"There are some nice tavern wenches, but I have seen no sign of any young misses running about, if that is what you mean. I daresay they will crawl out of the woodwork if they get wind of your presence."

"Then let them not get wind of it."

"They should not. I merely said I was one of your agents from London to see to your affairs." Emory sniffed as though he had fallen on his sword for his master. "We have kept only the small staff of the housekeeper, butler and cook, as you directed."

"Excellent. I can look after Goliath myself while I am here, for I do not intend to do anything else."

"It will do you good, your Grace."

"As I offered before, you are welcome to take a holiday. I know you have family hereabouts. I have no intention of leaving the property, so you will not be embarrassed by my appearance."

Emory gave him a mocking look as he began to help Hugh from his muddy boots. They had been together since his time at Cambridge so he was granted a great deal of impertinence.

"I would take leave of absence, but Watson has mentioned some odd happenings about the estate, and they are too aged to be of any assistance."

"Pray enlighten me." Although he did not particularly want to hear what he had to say.

"Most likely, I would not have been suspicious, but over a week ago there was a wreck of one of the Crown's ships and they believe it was intentional. The rumblings in the tavern are that a gang of gentleman are active again in these parts."

"Were they ever not?" he asked doubtfully.

"I could not say, your Grace, but I decided to ride about the property, and there are some fresh tracks down by the beach and old fishing hut. I did not find anything inside, so it could be no more than some curious youth wandering about."

"Indeed. You and I can ride down later and take a look."

"It would be a perfect location, however, with it being at the mouth of the River Leven where the headland overlooks the sea."

"Not to mention the fact that the owner is always absent, and the only servants are elderly retainers," Hugh added cynically.

Emory inclined his head.

"Your land agent told me that over the past few months there has been some small damage to fencing, and it looked as though someone was inhabiting one of the old cottages. Again, it could be a coincidence."

"Has anything been reported to the magistrate?" Hugh asked.

"Not to my knowledge, your Grace."

"You do know, Emory, that I am on holiday."

"Yes, your Grace."

"This Season was enough of an adventure for me."

"Yes, your Grace."

"Please stop 'your gracing' me."

"Yes, your Grace."

"You may go now."

"Yes, your Grace."

"I missed you too, Emory."

Hugh leaned back into the steaming water and relaxed his head over the edge. Perhaps a little adventure would not be such a bad thing. It would help him take his mind off why he had left London.

Maili curled up with a book in the large canopied bed in her room. She was not used to country hours yet. She would just now be going out for the evening, were they still in London. Fortunately, Brantley had an excellent library and she had found *Mysteries of Udolpho*, one of her favourite author's novels, to curl up with in bed. A nice gothic romance would not disappoint.

She was pulled into the story immediately when poor Emily lost her mother. Emily and her father travelled to Italy for respite and met a handsome stranger, who joined them.

"Where is my handsome stranger?" Maili asked out loud.

The family then received a letter that they were ruined, Emily's father died of illness and she returned home an orphan.

"Oh, I hate sad stories!" Maili wailed.

Fortunately for Emily, the handsome stranger, Valancourt, was there to comfort her and they fell in love.

"If only the story ended there," Maili said to herself.

Emily's new guardian did not care for Valancourt because he had no riches or social status, and whisked her off to Italy.

"Poor Valancourt. I am not poor, but I can understand his situation."

In Italy, multiple suitors attempted to win Emily—one even tried to steal her away through a secret passage! This caused Maili to take her taper around her room and check for secret entrances, but she found none. How disappointing!

The scheme was discovered, and there was a duel.

"How romantic!" Maili thought it would be nice to have two men want her enough to fight for her. "Ha! Even one would be nice."

Emily and Valancourt made their escape to the castle Udolpho, which was haunted.

"At least Castle Craig has no ghosts that I have found," she reassured herself as the story grew scarier. There was fighting, people were locked in turrets, and Emily saw a dead body before someone sneaked her out of the castle.

"Who was it?" Maili asked in frustration. "You cannot see a dead body and not tell us who it was!" she told the book.

Emily went away for a while, then returned to the castle. She inherited property and returned to France and was reunited with Valancourt.

"Happy ever after at last."

Several hours after she had begun, she closed the book with satisfaction and blew out the dwindling remnants of her taper. She lay staring at the canopy, but still sleep eluded her. The moon appeared to be a slight crescent, yet the light was streaming in her window. She threw back the covers and padded over to the window seat and sat there looking out.

She could not help but begin to think what she would do when she returned to Castle Craig. She had had some respectable offers, but for some reason she could not bring herself to accept them. Were Papa and Mama disappointed in her? They had not said so, but it was likely she would find no one better.

Could she be happy with a country squire or gentleman? She liked to think so, but why did she feel so disappointed in leaving London behind? She would never see many of those people again.

She was not a little bit disgusted with herself for wishing for more. She should be content and make the best of what she had. But now, did that mean she should apply to be a governess or companion? Her parents would never force her, but if she stayed at the castle, she would feel compelled to take the first offer of marriage that came along. Her stomach turned at the thought. She had seen enough of farm life to suspect what happened between man and wife and she could not imagine just anyone being her husband. She had experienced a kiss and it was tolerable, she supposed, but she would like her next one to be meaningful. The London flirts gave their kisses away too freely.

She looked out over the sea; the slight moon was leaving a brilliant reflection of itself in the rippling waves. She opened her window to hear the sounds of the water splashing against the rocks. It was still some way down to the sea from the house, but she could still smell the briny air and hear the gulls' screeches.

She was beginning to feel sleepy and she sat in the window seat listening to the sounds of the waves lapping and feeling the gentle breeze that blew in off the water. Her head bobbed and it woke her so that she sat up with a jerk. As she stood up to find her way to the bed, she heard male voices.

She strained to listen but heard no more. Her mind began to imagine all manner of sordid escapades. It only needed a Gothic castle with hidden, damp tunnels and dungeons.

"I might need to find some lighter reading before I retire," she told herself. She began to pull the windows in when she heard them again.

Should she alert her aunt and uncle?

No, for if she was wrong, they might be angry.

She threw on an old dark blue dress she could manage herself and wrapped her dark red cloak around her shoulders before she lost her courage. She tucked her half-boots under her arm, so as to be quiet on the stairs.

She would only try to get a peek and see what was going on. It could be nothing more than grooms up with a sick animal that she had heard, but she was too intrigued not to investigate.

She left the kitchen door on the latch and quietly stepped out into the darkness. She pulled on her half-boots as her eyes adjusted to the now cloud-covered moonlight. She walked towards the stables but there was nary a sound. She should return to bed, she told herself, but her feet were continuing to walk towards the sea.

If only she had not overheard her aunt and Mrs. Snodgrass talking about smugglers this afternoon, she would be able to leave it alone. She only wanted to watch anyway. She had no intention of confronting any men.

"Now, which way do I go?" she whispered to herself. The further away she got from the house, the more her nerves were on edge.

She found a small path which led towards the water and cautiously began to walk along it, though the pebbles crunched loudly beneath her soles. When she made it to a place where she could see the beach, she crouched behind a large rock. No one could see her there. It was a perfect hiding spot, though the beach was annoyingly devoid of trees.

She could see nothing and sighed with disappointment. She waited another half an hour, jumping at every little noise she heard, but there was nothing criminal to be seen. Who knew so many animals were nocturnal? Her legs were growing stiff, though, so she stood to return to the house. A large, gloved hand covered her mouth and pulled her up against a huge, hard body.

She was so afraid, she could not even force a scream from her throat. Not that it would make much noise with this leather glove over her mouth. When she tried to assimilate her wits, a voice growled quietly in her ear.

"What the devil are you doing here?"

CHAPTER 6

*H*ugh could not sleep. He and Emory had investigated the tracks out by the sea, but there was no clue as to any signs of a smuggling ring on his property. Still, something did not sit quite right with him.

He stood looking out of his bedchamber window. In daylight, it commanded a far-reaching view of the water towards Ireland. At this hour, there was only a sliver of moon occasionally showing between fast-moving clouds, and if someone were going to bring a ship in, it was a perfect night. His memory flashed back to the crew of Deuce and his comrades at the inn a few nights past. Could smuggling be what they were plotting? It would not surprise him in the least to know that Deuce had been responsible and was now leading a gang. But why here? It was not near enough to London to be an overly lucrative prospect... or was it? Hugh could not recall where Deuce hailed from; however, he would need to search *The Peerage* to see if there were any clues there.

The last incidents had been intentional wrecking of a ship carrying goods for the Crown. That was a much more serious offence and required inside knowledge of the Crown's movements. It would have to be worth the risk, so there must be something of value in it.

Smuggling itself was wrong, of course, but with the exorbitant taxes on tea, brandy, spices, and fabrics, it was difficult for ordinary folk to have such things otherwise. It had gone on as long as he could remember, and most people looked the other way. At times, smugglers were more akin to pirates, and if anyone informed on them they would suffer repercussions. Hugh was not concerned about that, but he was concerned about an operation occurring on his property without his knowledge or consent.

He began to pull on his trousers and boots. He could not sleep, so he might as well take a walk.

He meandered through the gardens for some time, trying to calm his restlessness. He began wandering down towards the sea, although not with any intention of catching the smugglers if he found them. He needed more time to plan a course of action. One man versus a dozen or more would be a disaster—if not a death sentence. However, if they were operating, he could observe and learn their habits.

He made it to the pebbled path that divided his lands from his neighbour's. He stopped still in his tracks when he thought he heard some voices, trying to determine their direction.

Of course, when I stop, they grow quiet, he thought sardonically. He took a few more steps as gingerly as he could, until he reached a place where he could see the beach and the old fishing hut.

He found a hiding place between two rocks and settled himself for a long wait.

He was about to doze off when he heard voices again. He sharpened his gaze on two men. It did not seem as though they were carrying anything, but one lit a lantern. Checking his watch in the moonlight, he noticed it was half past midnight. He wondered if a shipment would be coming in shortly, and realized he knew very little about smuggling. Most of his knowledge was from stories or fantastical tales men told in the clubs. Perhaps he should contact the local Revenue officer, but he would begin his questioning with his own retainers.

As he watched for the men to exit the hut entrance, he heard footsteps coming along the path. He was on high alert; at once, he placed a hand on the knife he kept strapped in his coat and waited to see what happened. Would the smugglers be so bold as to walk his own lands or that of his neighbour's? He was struggling to recall who was his neighbour here. He would have to ask Watson later and consider paying a call—though he dreaded doing anything social.

The footsteps grew uncomfortably close and someone stopped a few feet from where he stood. They seemed to be on a similar mission to him, since they crouched behind a boulder. He had no notion of who it might be, other than perhaps someone from the neighbouring estate. They wore a heavy cloak over their head, almost like a woman. Why would a female be out on the beach in the middle of the night, unless she was involved? He was quite curious as to whom his watching companion could be, and he strained his head to try to get a better glimpse.

Would it be foolish to speak to her? Probably, it would be best to wait until the smugglers left the shack again and the coast was clear.

He was growing bored, however, and it was difficult to remain still. Whatever could they be doing in there for so long? Maybe they were just vagrants and they would be there all night. It looked as though his companion agreed, for she pulled her cloak tighter and repositioned herself to grow more comfortable.

The clouds moved, allowing a small ray of light from the moon to shine through. The stranger turned her head and Hugh's breath caught in his throat. Could it be? Or was he imagining what he wanted to see? He crept closer as quietly as he could, and her scent of orange blossom and vanilla wafted up to his nose. Good God! Did she know how dangerous it was to be here just now? He could strangle her, himself... and whatever was Miss Craig doing in Westmorland, the very place he had come to in order to get away from her?

As if sensing his presence, she stood up and he swiftly stepped closer, putting one arm around her waist to pull her back down against him and one hand over her mouth to keep her quiet.

"What the devil are you doing here?" he whispered into her ear.

He could feel her stiffen and start to let out a scream, but then, for some reason, she seemed to relax. She must have recognized his voice.

Then she tried to turn in his arms. The insufferable woman did not know what she was doing to him.

"Be still!" he ordered in her ear. "There are people in the hut and I do not wish them to know we are here. Do you understand?"

She nodded her head.

"Can you be quiet if I remove my hand?"

She nodded again.

He dropped his hand but did not let go of her. They were wedged against a boulder in a very awkward position, and he was struggling to keep his composure. Everything he had left London to avoid washed over him, as if Satan were dangling a ripe, juicy apple before him. Trying to compose himself, he took a deep breath and forced himself to drop his hand from her and move back a little. She turned her face enough to look at him and all rational thoughts left his mind. His hands began to drift towards her face, if he could just touch her porcelain skin and taste those lips then perhaps he could forget her and be done. He tucked an errant lock of hair behind her ear, and her breath hitched as if she realized what he was about to do when they heard the men coming outside. His hand dropped as though burned by fire and he had to struggle to gather his wits.

~

Pure terror gripped Maili when she was seized. *It was the Count come to claim her!* She had thought immediately of the villain in the novel she had just finished.

Nonetheless, she had a suspicion her assailant was no would-be rescuer, and she was to be captured and chained in a fishing hut where no one would look for her.

Then she smelled the familiar scent of musk and spice and heard the deep whisper of the Duke of Cavenray. Could it be possible? But why was he on her uncle's property, hundreds of miles from London? He might loathe her, but he would never hurt her. Could he be involved in the smuggling? She attempted to turn to confront him but he held her still against his firm, lithe frame. She managed to turn her head to meet his gaze and he was staring at her with the look of a predator about to devour his prey.

Strange sensations swept over her—a frisson of anticipation and warmth, mixed with fear of the unknown. She had never been so close to a living male, and certainly not for so long.

It seemed as though he would kiss her, and she felt quite certain his kiss would be unlike the other she had experienced. Her heart stuttered and felt as though it lodged in her throat.

Her thoughts betrayed her and she blinked rapidly, trying to think through her muddled wits. She felt entranced by his look of hunger and was drawn forward by some force she could not seem to control. She was saved from herself when they heard the voices of men on the beach.

One of the men held a spyglass to his eye and scanned the area, perhaps on the lookout for the Revenue men. A light flashed from somewhere overhead and a minute or two later the men flashed the lantern from the fishing hut.

"That was from my property!" he exclaimed in disbelief.

Perhaps he was not involved, based on his exclamations. Thankfully, she had not yet accused him and made herself even more foolish in his eyes.

She and the Duke remained silent as they waited to see what would happen next.

Lights flashed back and forth between the people on land and the ship. It was likely to be no more than signals telling the ship where to land, but it seemed they were speaking a language to one another.

The lights stopped, and Maili could feel the Duke's breath on her neck; it sent a shiver through her and only made her feel more conscious of the danger she was in.

Out of nowhere, a boat being rowed by about a dozen crew slid through the water with barely a sound. They worked in perfect unison until they reached the two men who had come out from the hut to stop the boat and secure it. Swiftly the boat was disembarked and its cargo was unloaded as though part of a race. Half-ankers were hauled into the hut, along with a few trunks.

As soon as it was empty, the men climbed in the boat and rowed back to the ship. Maili felt like she could finally breathe, but Cavenray whispered in her ear again. "Shh. They might have another load."

"More?"

"Possibly. Sometimes they leave the goods out in the water until it is safe to bring them in. That way, if the Revenue Officer comes and catches them in the act, they do not lose everything."

"You seem to know a lot about this," she whispered back at him.

"I have been gaining an education from my valet today."

They grew silent again, and sure enough, another boatload of goods was brought in from some ship off in the distance.

When the crew had been sent back out to sea and the two men had departed, Maili again realized the peril she had placed herself in.

"That was fascinating. Good evening, your Grace." She made to walk away and he grabbed her arm. She looked down at his hand holding her.

"Where are you staying?" he asked.

Was he daft in the head? "At my aunt's house, of course."

"Your aunt?" he asked in confusion.

"Lady Brennan. You seemed to know her at the Seftons' party," she reminded him ungraciously.

She could see a flash of annoyance pass through him quickly before he hid it. Was he angry he had forgotten his neighbours, or that she was there with them? It was likely to be the latter.

"I will see you back to the house."

"You most certainly will not!" she protested.

"You may not think very highly of me, Miss Craig, but no gentleman would allow a lady to be out here unescorted with those dangerous men lurking."

She opened her mouth to protest because she wanted the last word, but she closed it again. She would feel better with him walking her back to safety, and suspected he would not allow her to win this argument.

Thankfully, he did not show any triumph on his face as he held his arm out for her. She chuckled at the formality after the precariousness of their past hour spent together. No matter. They walked forward in silence until they could see the stables. She tried not to dwell on the feel of his arm beneath her hand and she willed it not to shake. The last thing she wanted him to think of her now was that she was a coward.

"Do not tell anyone I am here, I beg of you, Miss Craig." The Duke stopped and turned to her, the words said with pleading eyes.

"It is too late, your Grace. At least, the vicar's wife said she had heard someone in the family was come here."

He cursed under his breath.

"I do not think they know it is you, however."

"Do you think you could meet me tomorrow afternoon?"

Her eyebrows raised at his suggestion.

"Do not give me a set-down, Miss Craig. If I had meant to ravish you, I easily could have done so this evening. I would like to speak to you further on this matter, but I would prefer not to be caught here at night with you, outside your uncle's home."

Maili hesitated. It was a very bad idea. And why would he want to speak with her? "Are you certain you could not call here? My aunt and uncle can be trusted."

"But their servants, most likely, cannot."

She blew out a frustrated breath. "Very well. My aunt enjoys a nap in an afternoon, around two o'clock. I could, perhaps, take a walk unnoticed."

"There is a folly just past the pathway overlooking the river, if you go to where our lands join, which is the pathway we took down to the beach. You continue straight until you run into it. You cannot miss it, and we will not be bothered there, I assure you."

Maili swallowed. That was precisely what she was worried about. "Until tomorrow, your Grace." She bobbed a curtsy and walked away and did not hear him whisper, "Hugh. I just want to be Hugh."

CHAPTER 7

*G*od has a wicked sense of humour.

It must be so, for Maili Craig to have been deposited in the very place he had come to forget her, Hugh reflected, as he sat in his dressing room late the next morning.

"You are brooding again, your Grace," his impertinent valet remarked.

"I am not brooding. I am simply tired. There were smugglers on the beach last night and I went to observe." He had also been awake for hours thinking of Miss Craig and how she'd felt in his arms.

"If you say so, sir." Emory was worse than his old nurse in making him feel like a small boy again.

"Are you not going to ask about what I saw?"

"I imagine you will tell me if you wish to, sir," Emory said in a sulky voice.

"Why did I bring you with me, Emory?"

The valet gave a dignified sniff as his answer. "I can leave today to visit my sister, your Grace."

"Stuff and nonsense, Emory. I will need your help to smoke these ruffians from their holes."

"What do you intend to do?"

ELIZABETH JOHNS

"I have not decided. I am hoping it will be easier to observe if my presence remains unknown. We will speak to Watson and Mrs. Sizemore today. You will have to spend more time with the villagers, being my eyes and ears."

"And what will you do?"

"Hopefully, remain incognito. I did happen to chance upon the neighbour's niece, who is an acquaintance from London."

"That is most unfortunate." Emory handed Hugh his breeches and shirt.

"Perhaps, but she is going to attempt to see if any information can be found at Brantley—discreetly, of course," Hugh answered, although he had his doubts about her *savoir faire* in that area.

"How many young ladies do you know to possess those talents?" Emory asked scornfully as Hugh tucked his shirt in.

"I hope she may surprise us. Gossip can often lead to good information, and ladies are quite talented in useless chatter. This lady is, in particular," he added derisively.

"Where would you like me to begin?" Emory asked as he helped his Grace into his waistcoat, then handed him a crisp neckcloth.

"Casually mention downstairs that you saw lights flashing last night. Act as if you are interested in purchasing some of the spoils—this is all about money, after all. Pretend ignorance if you must. Then try the tavern in the nearest village. If that does not ferret anything out, I know another village worth trying."

"Very good, sir." Emory helped him into his coat and Hugh shot his cuffs. "Will you need me back for anything else?"

"No, this is most important. I am dressed. I think I can manage for the rest of the day."

Hugh made his way to the breakfast table and pondered what he should do until two of the o'clock. He wished to question his land agent, but often the local people were heavily involved or looked the other way at the gentlemen of the night's activities. Often it was necessary to feed all the mouths they were responsible for. Hugh could not fault them for that. He finished his eggs, bacon and toast, then decided to take a walk down to the beach to see if there were clues to what was being smuggled and if it was worthwhile.

~

Maili heard her aunt's door click shut behind her as Lady Brennan sought her afternoon rest. She then checked her bonnet in the glass in the entrance hall before she left on her afternoon excursion. Ignoring why she had chosen her best walking dress of apple green and smart chip bonnet with a matching green ribbon, she at least felt she looked her best to meet again with the formidable Duke.

She had slept surprisingly well, despite her adventure the night before. Probably she had been exhausted from the excitement. Her dreams had been filled with a darkly handsome duke with black hair and midnight blue eyes, but she must be careful not to superimpose the dream on reality. In her dream, the man had held her in his arms and looked at her with adoration. In reality, the Duke looked at her with mocking eyes and spoke in clipped tones. How foolish she was to even let herself dream such things! She did not like the man!

As she grew closer to the sea, she found the pathway the Duke had spoken of, where they had trodden the night before. She never would have noticed the pathway the Duke had mentioned if he had not told her, but there was indeed another track that led away towards his estate. She hesitated before crossing over into his lands, but they did not seem as formidable in daylight. As she walked the path towards the folly, she wondered why a structure would be called a folly if it were not intended for such acts, then blushed. As if he would wish to do anything foolish with someone such as her. No. She lifted her head proudly and decided she would not let him make her feel inferior any longer. Regardless of her birth, which was now much better than she had thought, she was the same person and worthy. But why did he wish to speak to her?

Lost in her musings, she came upon the folly much sooner than she had anticipated. The view was breathtaking as she looked out over the sea, which was surrounded by mountains on one side and hints of the cottage's stone walls up on a hill to the other.

Their idea of a cottage was vastly different from her own. This cottage was a manor house as large as Lord and Lady Brennan's! The folly was a tower, really, and she was surprised she had not seen it from Brantley.

"Miss Craig?"

Maili started when she heard his deep voice say her name.

"Your Grace." She curtsied. "I was admiring the view."

"I was, as well," he said as though he meant her, not the sea. "It is a charming place. I cannot imagine why I have not been here in so long."

"It does seem a waste," she said before realizing her thoughts had escaped her mouth. Why was she so clumsy around him? She was confused—was he flirting with her?

"Indeed, it does. Do you always speak your mind, Miss Craig?"

"Not always, no." She had not come here to be insulted. She could feel her cheeks heat and dipped her head, hoping he would not notice them beneath her bonnet. He seemed to be assessing her, so she waited for him to speak, trying not to notice his casual elegance in his buckskins and gleaming Hessians. He wore a coat of dark blue to match his eyes and she wondered if he knew his effect, looking thus.

"Are you enjoying your stay?" he asked politely.

"Very much so, thank you. The Lake District is one of the loveliest places I have ever been."

"Have you travelled much, then?"

Did he make her feel small on purpose, or was it as accidental as the way her tongue was loose around him?

"I have not, your Grace. My travels are limited to Scotland and London."

"I have, and I would agree with your assessment of the area. There is little else that compares."

"Why have you asked me here today, your Grace? Surely, it is not for small talk. You had very little of it for me in London, if I recall."

"A direct hit, Miss Craig. You do not mince words."

"Forgive me, that was uncalled for. I am agog with curiosity as to why you would wish to speak with me."

He looked at her intently, and it took all her might not to wilt under his scrutiny. What was he thinking of when he looked at her so?

The Duke cleared his throat. "I came here to relax—a repairing lease, if you will. However, upon my arrival, it was brought to my attention that it was possible smugglers were using my absence as licence to use my property at their will. As you gathered last night, that is the case. What I wanted to know from you is why you were present on the beach? Have you any knowledge of this smuggling operation?"

"Are you accusing me of being involved?" she asked, affronted.

"I think that highly improbable, since this is your first visit to Westmorland. Yet what made you walk, unchaperoned, down to the beach last night, Miss Craig?" his voice asked accusingly. Who was he to question?

"I could not sleep and heard noises through my open window," she fumed quietly.

"So, you simply walked down to look, without any regard for your safety?"

"With all due respect, your Grace, you were the biggest threat I faced last night." She could bite her tongue out. Why had she said such a thing? Why would he care? Some misplaced sense of chivalry?

"I was never any threat to you," he snapped.

"Of course not," she retorted and turned to leave.

"Miss Craig, wait. I beg your pardon."

She stopped but did not turn back to face him, feeling affronted and also angry with herself for reacting to him.

"I meant no insult. Why do we have this effect on each other?"

She turned and looked at him with astonishment. She did not know whether to be flattered or indignant. She stood silent and stared at him. Why was he so handsome and intimidating? She had never felt so small in the presence of anyone else.

She then watched as he walked slowly towards her. Her breathing hastened and her pulse began to race impossibly fast. What was he going to do?

He held out his hand to her and she stared at it.

"Truce, Miss Craig?"

She let herself relax. "Yes, your Grace." She took his hand and felt a spark of awareness shoot through her—and immediately felt disgusted with her weakness.

He kept hold of her hand and she did not know whether to pull it back or leave it where it was. It was decidedly uncomfortable.

"Do you think you might call me Hugh while we are here?"

Maili's eyes shot up to his. "Are we to be seeing each other again?" she asked as she wrinkled her face.

She could sense his hesitation. "I did come here to rusticate, but I cannot imagine we will not meet from time to time, since our lands join. I also wanted to request you to ask, in an inconspicuous manner, questions about smuggling and to let me know if you discover anything."

"I, ask questions?" She pulled her hand away.

"Discreetly, of course. I would not want you to put yourself in any danger."

"And how am I to alert you of my discoveries? I cannot call on you."

"Well, you could, seeing as I only have a butler, housekeeper, cook and valet. But I do understand the proprieties."

She scoffed doubtfully. He looked at her with a humorous smirk.

"Come. There is a place in the folly where you may leave a message."

She took his hand without thinking and allowed him to lead her into the stone edifice.

CHAPTER 8

*W*hy had he suggested such foolishness? To deliberately tempt himself by being alone with Miss Craig was the height of madness. What was worse, she seemed perfectly suited to her surroundings here, whereas in London she had stood out. Not conspicuously, precisely, but she had not known how to play the game of the *ton* as she should. It was quite a ridiculous notion, that, and while it irritated him, it also intrigued him.

The trouble was, he found her more enticing in her comfortable habitat. He should remove himself immediately. Instead, he was drawn to her simplistic goodness, which had appeared to be a lack of sophistication amongst the hardened, jaded *ton*.

He watched her as she took in the tower, built some years before when it was fashionable to have useless architecture mimicking some ancient relic. This one could be useful, however, he thought, as he gazed upwards and began to wonder if it was not where the smugglers had signalled from last night. He would investigate after she left.

"Is this a lookout tower?" she asked, studying the spiral staircase leading upwards.

"I imagine it is," he replied.

"It would be a perfect place to signal from," she remarked, lifting her hand and feeling along the wall. There was a bench on the side opposite the staircase, but little else inside. She seemed fascinated, nonetheless. "May I go up?"

"Be my guest."

She scurried up the stone steps with excitement and he followed, trying not to permit his gaze to linger on her bottom for one hundred and twelve steps. She exclaimed in awe a few times about this and that. He imagined she was this enraptured with everything she saw. When had he become so numb to everything? He tried to view it as she was doing.

The view was quite impressive from the top—it was a three hundred and sixty degree panoramic of the sea to the west and the mountains to the east, with the river running just below to the north. The view he could not seem to take his eyes from, however, was standing at the wall, gazing out with wonder. He stepped up to the ledge next to her.

"Look at those boats going up the river. Do you think they are moving the goods from last night? They must have stored them in tunnels."

He looked down, and to his amazement, he thought she was right.

"You are probably correct. No one would suspect them in broad daylight."

"That is very clever of them. Do the boats have hidden compartments? I do not see any large barrels."

"They probably only move the smaller goods they can hide under the pretence of being fishermen. I would imagine those barrels would have to be transported at night by horse or mule."

They watched until the boat floated up the river out of sight. She turned and began to look around, walking over to examine the walls more closely.

"Are you looking for the hiding spot?"

"I am. Will you show me or must I find it on my own?" she asked, continuing to search the stones with her eyes.

"There is a panel hidden in the wall there." He pointed to it and showed her where.

She fingered the stone gently and discovered he spoke the truth. It was not a real stone. When she found the small catch, she pulled it and an entire section of wall opened up, revealing a small room.

"I never would have known it was there!" she exclaimed.

"That is the general idea," he muttered.

"It will do nicely. What if I do not find out anything?"

"I suppose your lack of correspondence will tell me so." He could not bear that either, for some unbeknownst reason.

"I think I will die of curiosity or boredom if I do not know what is going on," she confessed, looking at him with a sheepish smile.

His insides churned with anticipation, just when he had thought himself incapable of such youthful feeling. His was a sorry case indeed. What would she do if he kissed her?

"I suppose I could leave a message here for you, as well. How about we try to leave a note here by two every afternoon?" He rasped like a silly schoolboy with his first calf-love, leaving secret notes and having clandestine meetings. It was highly improper and highly seductive.

"Very well, I will play my best at being detective."

"I find one often only has to bring a subject up and people tend to prose on and on without having to contribute much oneself." His eyes met hers and a delightful blush came from her neck up to her cheeks. He had not meant to imply it was she.

She abruptly turned away. "Forgive me. I know I speak too much when I am nervous, and I always seem to be saying the wrong thing when I am with you."

"There is nothing to forgive," he said, stepping up behind her. He needed to reassure her, he told himself. He gently turned her toward him and tilted her chin up. He thought she would not look at him, but he would not kiss her unless she gave permission. He waited until her eyes met his and did not tell of fear, but curiosity. He leaned his head down and touched his lips to hers.

It had been so long. He felt he had waited an eternity to touch her – taste her. Instead of sating his hunger, he was ravenous for more.

Her lips trembled, but she took her hand and touched his face. He was undone by her innocence and reminded of it at once. It took all of his will power to pull away.

She looked up at him with a stunned naïveté and he very likely groaned out loud. He needed to get away from here.

Miss Craig recovered her senses and dropped her hand with an "Oh." And then, "I should be leaving, your Grace."

He was too astonished by his feelings to say what was proper and apologize, but he did not want to apologize. He wanted more. Never before had a kiss felt thus.

He opened his mouth to try to force the words out. "I —Miss Craig—"

"Please do not insult me by apologizing," she said over her shoulder, clearly shaken.

Had it affected her as much as it had him... or was she insulted?

"I hope I did not offend you," he answered quietly.

She shook her head and hurried away, leaving him standing there feeling confused.

~

Maili tried to remain calm until she was out of his sight. Then she ran until she came to the path to the beach and she scurried down until she found the boulder she had been hiding behind the night before. She sat on it and allowed herself to cry. She hated crying. Why did he affect her so much? She was certain the next words out of his mouth were going to be something disgraceful. The kiss she had received in London had been offered by a flirtatious rake, who had followed it with an offer of the dishonorable sort. She had never been so astonished. Then he had left – laughing at her when he had realized she thought he would consider her worthy of marriage.

So why, then, would someone as lofty as Cavenray? He would not.

If only his kiss had not been so devastating. It had felt nothing like the slobbery onslaught of lips she had suffered during the previous attempt by the rake, whose hands had also tried to wander.

There was only one solution. She would have to stay away from him and not allow it to happen again.

She pulled out her handkerchief, dried her eyes and took a few deep breaths of the fresh, sea air. He had asked for her help and she would give it. For one, what the gang was doing was wrong, and for two, it was a most exciting prospect to help catch them. Soon, she would be travelling back to Scotland for good and she would need these memories to help her through the remainder of her days.

Unobserved, as far as she was aware, Maili walked back to the house and slipped up to her room to refresh herself before tea.

How was she to discover information about illegal activities? She could not just stroll up to people and ask them if they were involved in smuggling. She did remember when the Bow Street Runners had been at Castle Craig, investigating when the vicar's wife had become crazed and tried to kill Margaux. But there had been several Runners, and they had had the authority to ask questions.

Her maid knocked and came in to help her change her gown.

"Did you have a nice walk, miss?"

"I did." Should she ask Lilly if she knew anything? She was a local girl whom her aunt had engaged for Maili while she was here. She had shared her mother's maid while in London. "It is quite beautiful. I walked down by the beach and found a hut."

"Lawks, there are fishing huts all about these parts," Lilly stated, pulling a pale blue sprig muslin day dress from the wardrobe and laying it on the bed.

"Are there?" The girl seemed a bit fanciful. Perhaps... Maili was certain her eyes must be giving her away, but ... "Do you ever have pirates here, along the coast?"

"Oh, none that I've heard of, miss; we just have the free-traders." Lilly pulled Maili's walking dress over her head and helped her don a fresh gown for tea.

"What are they?" Maili feigned ignorance. "It does not sound the same. Pirates sound so romantic!"

"Oh, but it is! They sneak things in on dark nights over the sea and hide them in the huts and caves and tunnels." The girl felt the need to defend her people, apparently, as she tied Maili's laces with exuberance.

Maili gasped. "There are tunnels on this beach?"

"Oh yes!" Then Lilly threw her hand over her mouth.

"What is it?" Maili questioned.

"We aren't supposed to talk about it to strangers, of course. You won't tell no one, will you?"

"Of course not, and I do understand. No mortal man can afford to pay the King's tax on anything."

That seemed to convince the maid.

"Well, I suppose you aren't exactly a stranger."

"I assume that is where most of the tea and brandy comes from."

She nodded. "Of course. Until recently, it were only small loads, but it seems since that big wreck they be wantin' the men to do more."

"Who are 'they'?" Maili asked as innocently as she could.

"Oh, I don't know. They keep that a big secret."

"It makes me think of some books I have read. What a mystery!"

"I wouldn't go trying to solve this one, miss. They be dangerous folks, not to mess with. Most of the men around here just help with the runs to supplement their pay, but the folk who interfere always come to no good."

"What happens?" Maili asked with open astonishment.

"Some have had their places burned or their animals killed. Rumour is, some have been murdered and they make it look like an accident o' course."

Maili exclaimed. "Oh!"

The girl had an impish look in her eye, ready to impart her juicy tidbits. She leaned closer and said in a loud whisper, "The rumour 'tis the ol' Duke were killed when he tried to interfere."

"The Duke of Cavenray?" Maili could not believe it. "How did he die?"

"He drowned and 'is body were found washed up on the shore."

Maili made a gasping sound that appropriately portrayed her astonishment. "How utterly and completely horrible!"

The maid nodded. "So, you see why no one talks. Besides, ain't no one rich enough hereabouts to pay them kind of taxes!"

"No, indeed."

"Do you need me for anything else, miss?"

"That is all for now, Lilly."

The maid closed the latch behind her and Maili sat at the small writing desk wondering what she should write to the Duke. She was not sure she had discovered anything he did not already know.

CHAPTER 9

*H*ugh decided it was time he tried to speak to the local Revenue Officer. Emory was to dispatch an invitation to the official to call at Gracemere this afternoon, and he assumed it would be accepted. Unless the man had no wits, he could be counted on for discretion.

Hugh directed for tea to be sent up when the man arrived. They might as well be civil.

Lieutenant James arrived precisely on time, as expected. Hugh chuckled as he pulled out his watch to see. The man had an excellent military bearing; no doubt he had recently been serving with His Majesty's Navy. The moustache was just as impressive with its thick wings and well-groomed tips.

"Please come in, Lieutenant."

The man strode into the study and clicked his heels, giving a slight bow. "Your Grace, I presume?"

"You did your homework. I was hoping Hugh Dickerson would be anonymous enough."

The man inclined his head and studied Hugh with a keen eye.

"Please take a seat; tea is on its way." He gestured with his hand to the brown leather chair opposite. "I would prefer to keep my presence quiet. I came here to rusticate."

"So, how may I serve you, your Grace?" James asked formally.

"Firstly, by calling me Hugh or Mr. Dickerson while I am here, in case we meet in public. Secondly, I should like to know if you suspect any activity on my lands."

The officer took a deep breath. "To be frank, sir, yes. However, the common smuggling is not what concerns me. Believe it or not, I understand most farmers and fishermen need something to help them by, and they mind their own business peacefully."

Hugh was surprised by this admission, but he kept his face impassive. "The wrecking?"

"Precisely. There was a gang several years ago with a similar *modus operandi*. The leader of the gang was thought to have been dealt with— there were even rumours of his death, though no body was ever found."

"And it seems he has re-emerged?"

"I highly suspect it is the same man."

"Do you have a name, Lieutenant?"

He shook his head. "Only a nickname: Captain Deuce."

Hugh suspected the same thing—but was it the same Deuce he knew of old? It would be too coincidental for there to be two men of the same name. He would search his *Peerage* as soon as the officer left. "Are there any clues to his real identity?"

"There are rumours he is of the gentry or nobility, sir. I have yet to tie him to any family. He is elusive. The only local aristocracy with property on the coastline are yourself and Lord Brennan."

"And without coastal property?"

"There is Lord Brougham and Sir John Hibbert, but they are some distance off. Sir David Douglas has property on the north side of the lake, but he is never in residence."

"I believe I was at school with him. He had no prospects of a baronetcy then, to my knowledge." So, it was the same Deuce.

"He was a younger son. His brother and family were killed in a

61

carriage accident. They were well liked in the neighbourhood and it was quite a tragedy, to hear tell."

"And tell me, Lieutenant, how do you think my estate is involved?"

"Your beach and tunnels, of course. You are known to be an absentee owner and it is a perfect location. It is difficult to catch them, to be sure, with the river on one side and a rocky beach that protects them on the other. We suspect they come straight from Ireland, so we cannot catch them coming north."

Hugh steepled his fingers together in thought as he listened.

"In addition, there are not enough officers to patrol as we need. Most of the villagers are involved and those who are not dare not speak against them."

"Do you have any plan in mind to catch this Captain Deuce?"

"He seems to be most interested in the large shipments. He is a greedy one."

"So, might you request reinforcements for the next large Crown shipment coming through?" Hugh suggested.

"It is a possibility. Yet I am not sure anyone would heed my word, based on suspicions," James said doubtfully.

"I suspect I might be of help in that department. Give more thought to it. I sent my valet to the tavern to see what he may over-hear. I imagine he will have more luck than you," Hugh added with a sardonic twist of his lips.

"Yes, your Grace."

"If I learn anything, I will send word again. Please keep me informed, if you will, and keep my presence to yourself."

"Yes, your Grace." The man clicked his heels and exited the room.

Hugh poured a glass of brandy and looked at it, appreciating the irony. There was no doubt where it had come from. He meant the villagers no harm, but if it was really Deuce who was involved, some-thing bad was likely to happen and he could not let its occurrence be on his conscience—or on his land, the blackguard.

He opened the terrace door and found a chair overlooking the sea. It would have been much more relaxing if he did not know that Maili Craig was at the neighbouring residence. For some reason, he felt an overwhelming sense of loneliness, and noticed the empty silence of only himself and nature.

~

Maili walked down the stairs to the drawing room feeling mildly guilty for her excursion to Gracemere. Had anyone seen her? The servants always knew everything, so probably someone had, but would anyone snitch on her?

She was most confused about why the Duke had kissed her. He had not made her feel like Lord Weston had. It had felt tender – almost reverent. Why would he do such a thing if he disliked her so? She had heard it was just the way men behaved towards any woman, although today he had spoken politely to her as he had done with most acquaintances in London, she had observed. It was all so perplexing, especially after he had been offended when she had indicated he was a threat to her. She had not felt endangered in the least when he had kissed her. In fact, she had been disappointed when it had ended so swiftly. Did that make her a wanton?

It had certainly made her curious. Part of her hoped he would be there when she went to deliver her report tomorrow. The other part of her hoped he would not. She was still afraid of him and his disapproving manner.

She could do nothing about it now, so why was she worrying? She would see if she could approach the subject of smugglers with her aunt, though she highly doubted she would unearth much information there.

"Good afternoon, Maili. Did you have a nice walk? Tea will be in shortly," Lady Brennan said as she looked up from her embroidery.

"I did, Aunt. Did you have a restful nap?"

"Quite. I rest much better here in the country than in London. I meant to ask you if you ride? We can provide you with a mount while you are here; you only have to ask. I am certain Brennan would be happy to show you where to go. It is quite safe here for you to enjoy such exercise on our land."

"That is good to hear, Aunt. I wondered if that was the case when I heard you and Mrs. Snodgrass speaking about the wreck and Revenue officers being in the vicinity." Was she being too obvious?

Her aunt frowned. "To be honest, there is and always has been some smuggling in the area, as with any village on the coast, but in general it is a harmless occupation the local people use to supplement their meagre incomes. I do not think any ill will befall you in the light of day, even if there are free-traders in the locality. The last thing they would want is to be seen and identified."

"Very well." Maili suspected she would get no more detailed information than that, but she would prod a little further. "Do they use your beach or is that area safe to walk upon?"

"Oh, it is quite safe. I do not think, as magistrate, Lord Brennan would tolerate any illegal use of his lands," she said with confidence. The door opened and the butler set the tea tray down before them.

"Would you pour, my dear?" Her aunt motioned towards the tray.

"Of course." She poured the tea and added milk, before handing the cup to Lady Brennan. "Who owns the neighbouring estate? The beaches adjoin, do they not?"

"It is one of many estates belonging to the Duke of Cavenray." Maili could feel her aunt's keen gaze on her, waiting to see her reaction. She tried to feign appropriate surprise, as her aunt would expect after their discussion about him in the carriage. Apparently satisfied, Lady Brennan continued. "You have nothing to worry about, however. He has not been here in an age. I am sure it has sad memories for him."

"What happened?"

"I do not know all the details, of course, but his father drowned in an accident when the two of them were on a fishing trip here. The new Duke has not been here since. I cannot comprehend why he keeps the place. I hear tell it is not even entailed."

"How terrible! I wonder what happened?"

"I do not know if anyone knows for certain. I was away at the time. The rumours were that the old Duke had a heart seizure and fell in, though there were some rather more malicious in nature. I suppose there will always be those who think patricide is worth the risk for a dukedom."

"There are rumours the Duke killed his father?" Maili asked, wide-eyed.

"Foul play was never suspected, to my knowledge, but you know how people will talk."

"No wonder he never comes back here."

"Perhaps he will sell the place. It has been left uninhabited for too long. I have little doubt, if there is mischief with a new gang of free-traders, they know very well there is no one in residence to keep them in check."

"I imagine it would be nice for you to have neighbours, as well."

"Yes," Lady Brennan said wistfully, "but I am not lonely. I do have friends in the village, even though they may not be of our status. There is plenty to do here to keep me occupied, though less now since the boys are away at school."

"I would like to meet my cousins, one day."

"And so you shall."

"And my uncle? Am I ever to meet him?"

Maili could see her aunt debating and wondered if she would put her off again, or ever answer her directly.

"Maili, your uncle David…" Lady Brennan began. "I do not know what to say. I know you suspect he cheated Seamus out of his inheritance. Perhaps he did. I do not know."

"Can you not ask him?"

Her aunt looked at her as though she was daft. She shook her head. "I expect you know nothing about him. David was always the one to take risks; it has always seemed to me he gets a thrill from danger."

"But that does not mean he intentionally sent us away," Maili reasoned.

"It is difficult to understand and perhaps I am being too hard on David. He has been gone some years now."

"What happened?"

"He had to flee after a duel."

"He killed someone?" Maili asked in disbelief.

"That was the suspicion, among other things. David was always up to mischief. I suppose it was difficult being a younger brother to Nigel, who always appeared perfect in comparison."

"So, my uncle David just fled and has not been heard from again?"

Her aunt looked at her blankly as if lost in thought. It was answer enough.

"Who has been managing his estate?"

Lady Brennan managed to refocus her thoughts and look at Maili. "An agent, I suppose. I have never enquired."

"I would very much like to go and have a look at the estate. Do you think my uncle Brennan would be willing to make an enquiry for me?"

"I can ask him," she said quietly. "I have not returned there since the funeral."

"Thank you, it would mean a great deal to me. I remember so little from that time."

Her aunt only nodded and wiped at the tears trickling down her cheeks.

CHAPTER 10

*M*aili penned her letter to the Duke and folded it when the ink was dry. She did not think she had learned anything useful, but she told him what she had found out, anyway. Part of her hoped to see him at the folly, but the other part of her was irritated that she felt this attraction to him when she was quite certain he was toying with her affections when no other females were at hand. She wondered if that was how it was for gentlemen. She had heard discussions about men feeling differently with regard to women; that for males, love was quite a separate thing from the physical act. Was it possible that love was what she was feeling? Never before had she felt her heart speed up and her insides flutter around a man. Mayhap reading romances was putting fanciful notions into her head.

She left the house and walked down the hill until she reached the pathway onto the Duke's land again, where she paused and looked around. There did not appear to be anybody watching and so she stepped forward.

When she drew near the folly, she heard voices and froze in place. Could there be smugglers having a meeting in the tower? Or could the

Duke be meeting someone else there? Perhaps he had brought his valet with him. She took a few steps back, found a hiding place behind a tree and debated what to do.

When she heard the voices again, she thought perhaps she should go a little closer to see what they were saying before making a decision. Two people were speaking: a man and a woman.

"But why are you here? It is not safe!"

Maili gasped. That sounded like her aunt.

"I do not think I am in danger. It has been years."

"Why meet here?" Lady Brennan asked.

"I am happy to see you, too. You look well after all these years. How many brats do you have now?" the man asked.

"This is not our land!" she protested.

"Our dear Duke is quite the absentee landlord, if you had not noticed."

"I had heard some of the family was expected soon," she informed him.

"Is that so?" the man answered in a bored drawl.

"Do be careful."

"I am always careful."

"Are you? Then why have you been away for so many years?" the woman asked suspiciously. "Where are you staying? At Crossings?"

"Here and there."

"I have it in mind to visit. It is less than fifteen miles. Would that be acceptable?"

There was a moment of silence and Maili wished she could see. The man could be no one else but her Uncle David.

"So long as you do not expect to be entertained. I am still not at home to visitors. I have business elsewhere at the moment. It is rather far to operate from." He sounded amused. Oh, to see his face!

"Has the property been maintained?"

"Well enough. I've a decent steward."

"Do you intend to stay, this time?"

"I never was suited to the country gentleman's life, Annie. You know that."

"It is just as well," she replied.

"What do you mean by that? Afraid I will tarnish your proper place in Society?" he snapped.

"I am scarcely in Society, but... never you mind. Stay out of trouble, this time."

"I do my best, sister."

"Please tell me you are not involved with the new gang wrecking ships— ships belonging to the Crown. There are Revenue men swarming along the coast since the wreck not two weeks past."

"I will not tell you, then."

"You will hang!"

"Only if I am caught committing a crime. I do not intend to be caught doing any such thing, so do not waste your worry on me."

"I cannot help you in this," she warned.

"Will not," he corrected.

"As you say... and next time, just send a message. I will not be trespassing on his Grace's land again."

"What he does not know will not hurt him. Everything is left as it was found."

"David, it does not have to be this way," she pleaded.

"Oh, but it does, sister. My time abroad has been very educational. If I play my cards wisely, I will be in my rightful place again soon."

"However do you propose that? What have you planned, brother?"

"Ye of little faith!" He chuckled. "Things are not always as they seem, sister mine."

"Of course they are not, but nothing good can come of deliberately sabotaging ships!"

"Tut, tut. Stop working yourself into a fuss. Soon you and I will not have to meet in secret places. Run along, now and keep mum that you saw me for the time being."

"David, there is family about here. If you heed none other of my warnings, I beg of you to stay away in daylight."

"I will take that into consideration, sis."

∾

"The devil, you say," Hugh muttered under his breath when he saw Deuce sneaking into the folly a quarter of an hour before Miss Craig was supposed to leave her note. He knew she had not been there yet, because he had checked twenty minutes prior and had stayed to watch for her. This could only mean she was going to be in danger if she happened upon that man.

He had not considered the blackguard would be so bold as to come to the lookout in broad daylight, but he should have known the Deuce of old would not have changed his colours. He had always done the opposite of what anyone expected.

Quickly, Hugh decided to move around the path where Miss Craig would approach and try to head her off. However, as soon as he stepped onto the path, he saw another person advancing his way. Instead of Miss Craig, her aunt, Lady Brennan, came into view. Hugh could not fathom what her business could be, but he decided to hide and see what happened. If he thought her to be in any danger he could then show himself.

He found a place behind a tree to watch for Miss Craig while Lady Brennan headed straight for the folly. He could hear her footsteps echo as she climbed the tower.

"What on earth?" he muttered. Was Lord Brennan involved in something nefarious? He never would have suspected it; in fact, Brennan was the least likely type to involve himself in anything scandalous, always touting the straight and narrow.

When he finally saw Miss Craig coming up the path, she looked curiously cautious as she approached. She must have heard the voices in the tower as well, for she stopped and hid herself. Hugh was impressed despite himself. He did think her a bit silly at times, in the way she carried on, but perhaps she only behaved foolishly in his company, as she had said. He had no notion of why that could be. He did not think himself so very intimidating. He would have to ask Emory later.

He watched her standing there hiding behind a large oak, her head tilted as she listened to Lady Brennan talk to Deuce. He was sorely tempted to approach her and wrap his arms around her as he had that night on the beach. He could not be sure she would not squeal and give them away, however, so he refrained.

While she listened to the two talking in the tower, he watched the emotions cross Miss Craig's face. Suddenly, many things began to make sense. Deuce was the uncle who had sent her and her siblings to the orphanage. Hugh had paid little mind when Miss Craig was speaking to her aunt that night in London, but now he was putting the pieces together. Her mother had been Margaret Douglas. If that was the case, then Miss Craig could be in danger. He continued to listen and noticed Lady Brennan did not mention her niece's presence. The omission was wise of her—perhaps she knew what her brother was capable of as well as Hugh did.

Yet what could he do to protect her? Did he want to involve himself?

He had to make a hasty decision when he heard Deuce and Lady Brennan coming down the steps from the tower. Miss Craig was well hidden, but if she chose to show herself and speak to them, she might be putting herself in harm's way. He felt the need to at least warn her. Again, he crept quietly to where she was and placed his hand over her mouth and his arm around her body. She tensed with fright, but he held her close.

"It is only I, please remain silent," he whispered in her ear.

She nodded, looking relieved, and he removed his hand from her mouth.

Holding her in his arms again, he felt his pulse race and his mind began to dwell on her soft curves and how well she fit against him. He cursed his response and disciplined himself to have sense when he needed to be alert for the situation at hand.

Lady Brennan and Sir David approached along the path from the folly. Hugh and Miss Craig remained behind the tree, still frozen for several minutes until the other two had passed, and their footsteps could no longer be heard.

Miss Craig turned to face him and looked up, her grey eyes steady.

He was ever so tempted to press his lips to hers again. She was becoming forbidden fruit he could not resist.

"We should remain quiet until we know he is gone. I suspect he will return down the pathway to the beach, but I cannot be certain," Hugh instructed.

"She did not tell him of my presence," Miss Craig remarked. She had noted that circumstance too, he thought, with a frisson of unexpected pride.

"I think she was most wise," he whispered again. "Come, follow me to a safer place." He took her hand without asking and began to lead her through the trees toward the house. He had no idea where else to take her, even though she would likely protest.

"Where are we going?" she asked quietly. "My aunt will be wondering where I am and send someone to look for me."

He stopped where he was. It was probable they were out of Deuce's hearing by now.

"I have put you in danger. Forgive me."

"What do you mean? I have put myself here, knowingly."

He shook his head. How could he explain this to her without insulting her uncle?

"I have known your uncle since our schooldays at Eton," he began.

"So you knew. Are you afraid of him?" she asked, searching his eyes.

How should he answer? "Your uncle..." He hesitated.

"Do not spare my feelings, I beg of you. My aunt has told me he is a dangerous man, one not to be trifled with. I notice she did not tell him of my presence and I can only assume it is to protect me."

"She has more sense than I would have credited her with."

"I suspect that is the case for most of my sex," she retorted.

"That was unjust."

She did not apologize but gave him a look of defiance. "Was it?" she challenged.

There was something about Miss Craig when she behaved thus which drove him mad with desire. "Very well, I confess to being surprised when a female shows she has wits. You must understand it is *de rigeur* within the fairer sex to pretend idiocy."

She inclined her head. "Only amongst the *ton*, which is why I did not take in London."

"I would hardly say you did not take," he argued.

Again, she looked at him with a challenge in her eye, as though to argue over the compliment he had paid her, but she did not.

"I suppose it is pointless to discuss it now."

She pulled a note from her pocket and held it out to him. "I suppose this is also pointless now," she started with a half smile. A delectable dimple appeared in her right cheek.

"Have you anything to report?" he asked, trying to keep his mind from straying.

"Very little, I am afraid. My maid was quite open about the fact that smuggling is a common occurrence on any coast in England. My aunt also acknowledged as much, but she vehemently denied my uncle Brennan's involvement in any way, since he is the magistrate."

"Which clearly proves his innocence," Hughes said sardonically. "Although I am inclined to agree, from what I know of Brennan. He is as strait-laced as they come."

"That is the extent of my discoveries for my first day," she said as she held up her hands expressing finality. "Have you fared any better?"

"I met Lieutenant James. He is the Revenue officer."

"And?" she prodded, a look of impudence lighting those grey eyes.

"Impatient imp," he chided, to hide his appreciation. "I made it clear to him I am at his service. However, I told him my wish is not to harm the common labourer only wishful to feed his family."

"And how did he react to that?" she asked with apparent interest.

Hugh tried to keep a straight face at her artless curiosity. She was beginning to tempt him in a different way from before. He cleared his throat to pull his mind back to the present. "He seemed to understand. I discussed setting a trap with him. I think I might be of use to him with my connections to the Crown."

Miss Craig stood quietly, worrying her lip in the oddest manner.

73

She seemed to be thinking. "Do you mean to have my uncle killed, then, sir?"

"I do not mean to have anyone killed. If that is a consequence of his chosen occupation, then I cannot be blamed for it."

"Of course not," she agreed. "However, it does seem a shame to lose him without knowing him."

It was Hugh's personal opinion the man was not worth knowing, but he refrained from saying so.

"Was he not the one who had you sent to the orphanage and assumed your brother's rightful place as your father's heir?"

"I have not had the opportunity to ask him if that is how it happened, but it is logical to assume that is what occurred," she said morosely. For the first time, she looked downtrodden. Hugh cared not one bit to see Miss Craig sad, and he was the one at fault for making her thus. He reached out and placed his hand on her arm.

She did not look up and he feared she was going to cry. He placed a finger under her chin and lifted it. Her large grey eyes were indeed threatening tears and he could not bear it. He placed his lips to hers to kiss away the melancholy, but he soon forgot why he had started the caress.

Before he knew it, his hands were holding her face, and then his arms were wrapping around her and drawing her close. Her lips were soft, luscious and tasted faintly of honey.

"Why do you keep doing that?" she asked candidly when he finally came to his senses and pulled away.

"Self-torture has become a hobby," he muttered. "I think you should avoid the tower in the future," he added, changing the subject.

"Do you think they will continue meeting here since she warned him?"

"Perhaps not, but I cannot put you at risk."

"How else am I to contact you if I have information?" she asked, with an adorable sideways tilt of her head.

"Very well. I or my valet will ensure the coast is clear before that time and intercept you, as I did today."

"I will be careful," she assured him.

"Yes, you did quite well this time." He eyed her knowingly. Her cheeks flushed in becoming response.

"Thank you. I must return before my aunt notices my absence." She turned and hurried away, while he stood there pondering whether he should choose to maintain his sanity and leave, or stay and help capture Deuce.

CHAPTER 11

"There you are, Emory. Did you learn anything?" Hugh asked, looking up from the book he was attempting to read. He glanced at the clock on the mantel; it read half past three.

"I sat there so long I could barely feel my legs," Emory replied, somewhat peevishly.

"Help yourself to a drink and tell me what you discovered." Hugh waved to the decanters on the table.

"I think I will pass on the drink, thank you, sir. In fact, I will be happy to not see another drink for a month. Those men could make a fish feel waterlogged."

"I suspect they were pleased to have someone else paying for their ale."

"Aye, and I doubt if there will be much work accomplished in the village today."

"Well, was my coin well spent?" Hugh asked.

"Very tight-tongued when sober, they are."

"But loose-tongued when not? That is a trait of any class," Hugh remarked.

"It was as you suspected. The original gang has returned. They are all strangers, operating under a leader from the local gentry. Details are kept very secretive. Rumours and suspicions abound, but no one has any proof," the valet explained.

"Sir David Douglas?"

Emory nodded. "No one would say the name, of course, but Captain Deuce is the moniker he is known by."

"Was there any word to explain the long absence?"

"He was thought to be dead," Emory said succinctly.

"Really? I wonder why I never heard a word of it."

"Perhaps because it happened at the same time as your father's death. As the legend goes, there was a duel and he killed the other man; then there was a bad storm when he was making his escape. The ship and other men were found, but he was not."

"How utterly convenient for him," Hugh muttered. "And now he returns years later hoping everyone has forgotten."

"One would assume so."

"How do the villagers feel about this operation? Are they hoping to become part of it or do their sympathies lie with us?"

"I did not sense any particular affection for the gang."

"I assume everyone knows they are operating from Gracemere."

"Naturally."

"The question is, do they assume I am aiding and abetting Douglas or do they think he takes advantage of my absence?"

"I would say they are split in their opinions. Does it matter, sir?"

"That remains to be seen. Some also say I killed my father, so if they believe that they may believe I condone Deuce's activities."

"You are aware they say such things? I would not give a fig for their opinions," Emory said snobbishly, his nose wrinkled with distaste.

"No, doubtless you would not. However, it could matter when we need to remove Deuce from his lofty perch."

"You intend to see this out?"

"I do. It is something I should have dealt with long ago."

His valet said nothing. Indeed, what could he say? He knew nothing of Hugh's history with Deuce.

"One last thing. Was there any word to indicate when the next run will be?"

"There was a lot of speculation and grumbling about the gang interfering with local runs, but no word on when they are or how regular. I suspect Deuce lets them know when one is expected."

"Yes, I suppose it cannot be precise."

"Do you require my assistance tonight?" the valet asked wearily.

"No, you may go to bed. You look horrid. Besides, I have some letters to write."

"I look as I ought for being up half the night, plying the locals with drink," he replied indignantly.

"As you say. Rest well, for I have another task for you tomorrow."

"I cannot wait, your Grace," he replied with a testy bow.

Hugh chuckled as his valet left the room. He found he was actually enjoying himself for the first time in years. He tipped his head back over the armchair and closed his eyes. Now that his suspicions were confirmed, how was he to deal with it whilst maintaining his anonymity? Should he reveal himself in order to keep Miss Craig safe? Perhaps he should, but not just yet. She needed to be protected from her uncle, and for now he thought he could do that best by keeping his presence a secret. He was playing with fire—if he was caught pursuing clandestine meetings with her, he would need to marry her. The thought did not frighten him as perhaps it should.

Could someone die from boredom? It had been five days since Maili had found any new information to take to the Duke. To make matters worse, it had been raining without pause as well. She had never been content to sit idly and this was testing her last nerve. She was certain it could have nothing to do with the handsome Duke who was hiding away on the neighbouring estate. It was hard not to get ideas above her station when he kept kissing her, and making her wits go begging. It was quite unkind of him to tease her so. Most likely, he would pay her no mind if they were back in London, and she would do well to remember that fact. Still, she was beginning to think better of him and it was exciting, being privy to his whereabouts when no one else was.

There had not been any activity on the beach that she could tell from her window, and she did not know who else to question for information. It was quite disappointing. She wanted to help solve the mystery and be part of the adventure.

She looked out of the window at the cloudy sky. Would it rain again today? She had to leave the house, one way or the other, or she might burst from boredom. Perhaps her aunt would take her to her childhood home today.

She made her way down to the breakfast room, hoping her aunt would join them, for she was excited to ask, but Lady Brennan was not there. In fact, her uncle informed her Aunt Brennan was taking a tray in her room.

When she had finished her own meal, she decided to check how Lady Brennan did, and tentatively knocked on her aunt's bedchamber door.

"Come in," she heard her call.

"How are you, Aunt? My uncle Brennan said you were taking a tray in your room and I wanted to make certain nothing is amiss."

"I have the headache a little, is all," her aunt confessed. "I know you had hoped to visit Crossings today, but I do not feel quite the thing and would not be a good companion."

"Perhaps I shall go for a long ride, then. I need to blow away the cobwebs," Maili said with a smile.

"Ask your uncle for my mount, Pecunia. She would suit you—we are of a size—and I know she needs the exercise." She reached over and pulled the bell. "I will have the horses readied for you. Do not stay out too long or you will be forced to spend the night and that would never do. It is easy to lose track of time out here."

"I will be careful. Thank you, Aunt." Maili leaned over and kissed Lady Brennan on the cheek before she left.

Maili was pleased with her aunt's mount. She was a spirited mare who needed a good gallop. Her uncle had told her of some scenic rides and provided an older groom for escort who knew the area well.

Maili headed northward. She had investigated *The Peerage* and her uncle's maps in the study and so had a fair idea of where Crossings was located. She might not make it the whole ten miles as best she could surmise, given the condition of the ground after all the rain, but she would try her best.

"We can pass through Gracemere lands. The family is never in residence and the retainers are all so old they will never hear or see us," the groom said, drawing alongside her when he saw the direction she was taking. "It is some of the best land hereabouts for riding."

She nodded. Normally, she would be more cautious about making free with the Duke's land, but he knew she was here and she did not think he would mind—especially since it was partially to aid his efforts in stopping the gang. "I have heard it said the free-traders make good use of it," she remarked casually, taking the opportunity to see if the groom would share any information.

"Aye, that they do," he agreed, as if it were common knowledge, which it appeared to be. Unfortunately, he offered nothing further.

"The lands are vast for a summer residence," she mused. The other side of the estate was surrounded by mountains and more barren. They were able to gallop the horses with complete abandon and it was exhilarating. She had not had such exercise since leaving Craig. When they drew rein, she allowed her mind to travel back over all that had happened since then.

Her instincts were telling her that her aunt was hiding something else. She was inclined to like her, but so much remained unexplained. Perhaps she would keep mum herself, if her brother was a smuggler. What would make a gentleman like her uncle David become involved in illegal dealings? He was from a good family and would certainly have had good prospects—especially after her father had died and Seamus had been prevented from inheriting.

Was this legacy not enough, when he saw his peers become lords, then to inherit vast wealth and estates? That must be it. Maili enjoyed the prosperity she had been born into, but she had also been happy at the orphanage. Whatever the motivation, he had chosen the path of skullduggery and it had doubtless led him to falsifying her own and her siblings' deaths.

Was there a chance he did not know they were alive? Her aunt must think so. Whoever could have guessed they would be adopted by a baron and brought out in Society? She supposed she should be grateful. If, indeed, he had known they had survived, at least her uncle had left them to be raised as orphans and not killed them.

They reached the edge of the lake and rode along the pathway beside it for a few miles. They stopped along the lake's edge to water the horses and rest for a few minutes.

"We have just now reached the northern edge of the Gracemere estate," the groom remarked.

"We have been on the Duke's land the entire time?" Maili asked as she appreciated the view of mountains across the lake.

He nodded. "Are you ready to turn back?"

"Oh, no. I mean to go to the north side of the lake."

"To Ambleside?" he asked with obvious surprise.

"It is where I was born. Do you mind?" Not that she intended to turn back if he did.

She could tell he was trying to keep his face impassive, but she saw a mix of emotions cross his features. Was it fear she saw?

"As you wish, miss," he responded at last. "My lord said to follow you where you wished to go." There was a mild note of resignation in his voice.

"Excellent," she replied as she waited expectantly to mount her horse. He held his hands for her to boost up to the saddle and then followed her as she went on her way.

By the time they arrived at Crossings, it was later than she had hoped, likely well past noon. She knew her aunt and uncle would have disapproved if they had known her intended destination, but now she knew where it was, she thought she could accomplish the journey faster if she wanted to do it again. She fully intended to turn around when they reached the estate, but the groom dismounted.

"We should return at once. It is much later than I thought it would be." And she was too nervous to go in. What would she do if she happened upon her uncle?

"We have to rest the horses, miss. Besides, I know this estate well. We can get the horses a drink."

"Oh, very well. I did wish to have a look around, but I wanted to wait for my aunt to be with me."

"There's no harm in you looking around. No one lives here except a butler and a housekeeper, and I know both well. I will apply to them."

They walked the horses through the gates and up the path. Maili begin to recognize her home with those senses that aid memories. The sounds, the smells, the sights... it was almost too much to bear. Flashes of imagery came to her: of running through the gardens in pinafores with Catriona; of picking apples and making daisy chains. The swing by the water still hung from the old oak tree. She could almost see her parents' faces when the family had enjoyed a picnic there.

Sadness and longing filled her heart and she began to cry. She threw her hand over her mouth to cover her emotion but it would not do. She ran away from the groom, who had discreetly withdrawn with the horses to the stables. She ran as though it would make her pain go away; she ran until she reached the lake with her sides aching.

"Why? Oh, Mama and Papa, why?" she cried out.

So many memories she had thought were lost came back to her. How had she repressed them for so long? It had been almost twelve years since she had been here.

Her feet took her on a mindless tour around parts of the property she remembered. She found the small chapel and the family graveyard which stood next to it. There, in front of her unbelieving eyes, stood a large monument to her entire family.

Sir Nigel, Margaret, and their beloved Seamus, Catriona and Maili Douglas, taken from this earth to be with their Saviour far too soon in the year of the Lord, 1814.

She ran her fingers over the letters lovingly and in disbelief.

"What happened that day?"

She squeezed her eyes shut, hoping to summon memories from the accident, but she could remember nothing. Seamus and Catriona only had pieces of memories from that fateful day themselves.

She had lost all sense of time and the sun looked to have moved far into the afternoon. She began to walk back to the stables; not wanting to leave, feeling as though a large part of her, and many unanswered questions, remained there at Crossings.

CHAPTER 12

*H*ugh watched Miss Craig fly by on a dappled grey mare, with a groom following discreetly behind. Where in the world would she be going in that direction, and why across his land? Perhaps she felt free to use his estate or she did not know it was his. But the groom surely must do so. Not that Hugh minded in the least. No, he was admiring the view much more than he ought, as was becoming the norm. Her dark blue riding habit accentuated her glorious red hair, which was untidy from the wind in her face.

So, against all rational reason, he urged Goliath forward and followed at a distance. Could they have the same destination in mind? After she continued northwards along the lake, he assumed they did. It was decidedly difficult to follow her at certain times, for there was nothing to shelter behind. However, she did not turn back to look and neither did the groom. He would dismiss that groom if he were in his employ. The whole purpose of the groom was to protect her and watch their surroundings. Hugh could have overtaken the man and had his way with Miss Craig before the man had noticed. Or, more likely, a wild animal could.

Now his imagination was getting carried away. He prayed he had a response to his enquiry soon, so this whole mess could be over with and he could remove himself from temptation. No matter his best intentions, she was always there and he could not resist her.

He eventually saw her pull up before the gate at Crossings and hesitate. It seemed as though the servant was convincing her to go in by watching their body movements.

"What the deuce is he doing? Don't force her to go alone," Hugh snapped.

Of course, she went in.

Hugh was uncomfortable riding his beast in through the gates, in case anyone should be home. He knew that Deuce had said he was not living there, but his answer had also been evasive.

He walked Goliath to the edge of the lake to give him a drink and then tied him up to a nearby tree. He debated whether to follow Miss Craig into Crossings, but she could be in peril. She had known she was in possible danger when last he had talked to her, so why had she come here alone? It made little sense. He felt compelled to follow her. What if Deuce came back and found her?

"Women. No, this woman. Most ladies never would have thought to do such a thing." He shook his head. He should turn around and go back to Gracemere and mind his own concerns. So, of course, he looked around and cautiously entered into enemy territory.

Hugh watched from a distance as Miss Craig and the groom appeared to be heading for the stables. He began to dart from hiding place to hiding place along the outskirts of the property to keep her in sight, feeling like a buffoon. He could see the headlines now: *Duke Caught Stalking Mysterious Lady*, or *Duke Caught Trespassing Trying to Save Lady from her Family*, or some such horror.

But what else could he do? He knew very well what David Douglas was capable of— more than most—and he suspected worse. Therefore, he felt responsible for Miss Craig. If truth be told, her aunt should be responsible, but she seemed timid around her brother and would likely yield to his schemes.

He caught up with them just as Miss Craig was separating from her groom at the stables. She walked alone towards the lake, looking dazed.

Had something happened to her?

He observed as she sat in the swing and absent-mindedly began to sway back and forth, and twirl around. She faced away from him for some time, yet he dared not move closer and reveal himself. He was intruding in a most ungentlemanly way, but there was little he could do at this point. When the rope untwisted and she faced him again, she was overcome with tears and her shoulders were shaking with grief. He wanted to rush over and comfort her, but he dared not.

Then she jumped off of the swing and began running. He followed, knowing he was conspicuous, but there was little place to hide. He felt exposed and did not know how he would answer if she saw him. She stopped at the small graveyard and he saw tears rolling down her face as she fingered a headstone. It probably belonged to her parents.

Catching a movement from the corner of his eye, he started. He struggled at first to focus across the distance, but then he saw him. Good God above, what was he to do? Deuce was not supposed to be here!

He could do nothing yet. He had to wait and see.

Miss Craig began walking straight towards the blackguard. Had she seen him also?

Deuce came out from the gardens and began walking towards her. He had cleaned himself up since Hugh had seen him at the tavern, wearing buckskins and Hessians and a well-tailored coat. He looked every bit the country gentleman.

It appeared she had not noticed him, for she then jumped in surprise and froze where she stood.

~

Startled, Maili saw a man walking towards her. She was terrified. She had been caught red-handed, trespassing, and she did not know what to say.

"Good afternoon," the gentleman said as he grew closer. "Allow me to introduce myself. I am Sir David Douglas. To whom do I have the pleasure of seeing before me?"

Maili was too stunned to speak. He looked a mixture of her brother and the pictures she had seen of her father. He had the startling grey eyes they all possessed, but he wore a beard. He could not be much older than Seamus, but his face showed weathered skin and lines around his eyes. He was tall and muscular, more like a labourer than a gentleman, though he was dressed like a squire in buckskins and a well-tailored coat. She realized her mouth must be hanging open and she snapped it shut. Should she say something or run straight for the stables? Would he be angry she had come here? He seemed very pleasant.

"I did not mean to alarm you," he said gently.

"I was told you were not at home. Please forgive me," she squeaked.

"There is nothing to forgive," he answered with a smile. "May I assume you are one of my brother Nigel's daughters? You look exactly as your mother did."

Maili nodded. There was no sense denying it.

He held out his arm to her. "What an unexpected surprise. Please do come inside. I am certain we can rustle up some tea."

"Oh! I fear I must return, sir. I did not tell my aunt my destination and she will be worried if she awakes from her nap and I am not back."

He raised his eyebrows. "You came all the way from Brantley, alone?"

"Indeed not, sir. A groom is waiting for me in the stables."

"Let us go and speak to him, then." He led her by gently guiding her elbow forward and she went along, not knowing what else to do.

"Gibbons! How are you, old chap?" David looked at Maili as they walked into the stable yard and found the groom rubbing down her mare. "Gibbons worked for my family before he went with Annie, upon her marriage to Brennan," he explained. "Ride on back and tell my sister that my niece is taking tea with me and then I will escort her to Brantley myself."

"Yes, sir." Gibbons flashed a hesitant glance at Maili, but gave a small bow and followed the order.

Maili looked heavenward, wishing she could receive some divine guidance. She did not want the groom to leave her, yet neither did she wish to offend her uncle, and the chance to see her old house and learn more about him was too tempting.

"A cup of tea would be welcome, sir. I promised Aunt Brennan I would return before dark, however."

"Of course," he agreed.

They walked back to the house and entered through the kitchen, where the smell of fresh bread and roasting meat reminded her of being in that very place and sitting at Cook's work-bench, waiting for a treat.

"I am rarely here, so retain few servants. The fare is simple, but enough for a bachelor."

"I do not want for anything, sir."

"Mrs. Hibbard, may we have some cake and tea for the lady? I will be accompanying my niece back to Brantley and may not return for dinner."

"Of course, Sir David." She cast a glance over Maili.

Maili did not recognize the woman. She did not think Mrs. Hibbard had been in service when her family lived here.

"Would you like to take a quick look around?" he asked. "Very little has changed."

"I would like that very much," she replied. "I confess myself curious." She would also like to quiz him and have him explain what had happened, but he was being kind and she wanted to see the house.

He led her up the servants' staircase to the main floor. She immediately shivered; a strange eeriness had come over her, and she felt queasy and anxious.

"Are you cold?"

"Oh, no, sir. It is just unnerving to be here again."

They walked through a dark-panelled hallway until they reached the entrance hall with a grand, wooden staircase. Scenes of sliding down the banister with Seamus and Catriona came to her mind and she could not help but smile.

A parlour, a dining room and a study opened off the entrance hall, but they were shrouded in Holland covers. She began to feel scared, being alone in this empty, dark house with a stranger whose reputation was suspect. All of a sudden, she wanted to leave, but there was one more place she wished to see before she left.

"Is the nursery still there?"

"I have not touched a thing."

Her feet carried her up the staircase and down the hall past her parents' apartments to where the back staircase led to the nursery. She did not consciously walk there but her body seemed to know where she was going, almost as though she were watching herself in a dream. Part of her wanted to look into her parents' rooms, but it was likely Sir David was residing there now and she could not bear to see it changed. When she reached the nursery, her breath caught in her throat. She could see herself there as a child. She could hear her own laughter and that of her siblings, and she could see their old nurse, Smitty, sitting there in the rocking chair as if it were really happening. She gingerly ran her hands along the shelves of toys and walked over to the small room where her bed had been. Her pink coverlet was still in place, with her doll sitting atop staring at her.

"We were told you were dead," she heard her uncle's voice say and she snapped back to the present.

She slapped her hand to her chest and could feel her pulse racing. "I forgot you were there," she explained.

"I cannot imagine what you are feeling just now," he said kindly.

"Who is buried in those graves?"

He paused before answering. "I never looked in the caskets," he finally responded. He seemed uncomfortable.

She nodded blankly. He seemed in earnest, and why would he have looked in there? She was so confused and she wanted to get out of the house as quickly as possible.

"We should hurry. It is getting late." She hastened through the nursery back to the stairs and down to the kitchen as hastily as she could. There were two plates of fresh cake and tea waiting for them. David joined her and they began to eat in silence. She did not know what she thought she should say to him. Should she wait and see what he did next? He had not asked about Seamus or Catriona. Did he already know? His reaction to her was not as her aunt's had been. He had not been shocked to see her in the least.

CHAPTER 13

*I*nsufferable female! What do you think you are doing?"
Hugh muttered as he watched Miss Craig go into the
house with Douglas. He was being charming and would deceive her,
no doubt.

Now Hugh would be left outside like a fool for hours, waiting to
see what happened, yet he felt obliged to stay. The idiot groom had
abandoned her here all alone with that monster!

Glancing upward, he saw the clouds were beginning to darken. All
the day needed was a storm. Chivalry was most overrated.

He decided to wait on the far side of the stables, so he would be
near to Goliath when the time came to leave. He refused to contemplate that Miss Craig might not leave tonight. He had no plan for that
circumstance. Surely, she could not be so stupid as to consider staying
here!

It was near to an hour later when he finally saw them making their
way towards the stables.

"Thank God!" he exclaimed. He was growing tired and hungry.
The clouds looked more ominous and he had no doubt they would
cross Gracemere lands to have any chance of reaching their destination before the rains came down. He hurried to his stallion.

As Miss Craig came galloping past him with Sir David following, he waited to follow, and silently hoped she would lead Deuce a merry dance all the way back to Brantley.

From a distance, he admired the way Miss Craig sat and handled the horse with apparent ease. There was a wildness—something untamed—about her which continued to drive him mad. He wanted her now more than ever, and he was beginning to forget why he had objected in the first place.

They skirted the lake at a fast clip and reached his lands in about an hour. As he had suspected, Deuce jumped the fence without hesitating. What he did find interesting was that every time Deuce attempted to pull alongside Miss Craig, she would forge ahead as though she had not noticed.

He liked her more and more.

Unfortunately, the weather did not hold. The rain began to pour down in sheets from the threatening clouds and there was little place for shelter. He feared he would be seen since they were on the more barren, mountainous side of his estate. Hopefully, if Miss Craig or Deuce looked around, the rains would be too heavy for them to identify him. Fortunately, they did not look. Deuce was heading somewhere with purpose and Hugh suspected it was to one of the cottages or huts.

Where was he himself to go?

He should turn Goliath and head straight to the stables. There would be no shelter for either of them, but of course he followed, and watched as Deuce chose the folly. Had he no sense? Why did he keep asking himself ridiculous questions? He could be nursing a brandy in front of a warm fire at this very moment. He tethered Goliath to a tree not far from where they left their own horses and watched as they ran into the tower with the clear intention of waiting out the torrential downpour. He cursed, then sneaked around the outside of the folly, attempting to find a place to eavesdrop. A loud clap of thunder nearly caused him to jump out of his boots.

Thankfully, he heard loud footsteps on the stairs, so he dared to creep inside the door for a moment, to listen.

"I am not certain we should go to the top," he heard Miss Craig say.

"It will be all right," Deuce reassured her.

"What about the lightning? Does it not usually strike tall things?"

"I suppose it does, on occasion, but we should be safe enough inside."

Hugh heard two sets of footsteps continue up the stone steps and he breathed a small sigh of relief. He did not wish to go back out into the storm. However, Miss Craig was correct, they were a target in the tower. It had been struck before.

"Are you quite certain we should be here?" Miss Craig asked again. "It is one thing to ride across someone else's land, but to trespass inside..."

"I know the owner. He is never here to mind, even if he knew," Deuce said in scathing tones.

"I see. You do not like him."

"I like the fact that he is absent," Deuce replied. Hugh heard him stomp up another flight of stairs.

"Do you know the Duke of Cavenray well?" she asked.

"I suppose you could characterize it so. We were at school and Cambridge together, though we did not run in the same circles, nor see eye to eye." The last was murmured so Hugh barely heard it over the rain.

"Was he unkind?"

"He was your typical pompous, privileged, entitled aristocrat."

"I suppose it must be hard to be amongst people like that." Sensible girl, she was placating him.

"You suppose correctly. The rest of us have to make our own way, but you would not know about that, now, would you?"

"I understand more than you might think. I lived in an orphanage for a few years, and then I had the fortune to spend the recent Season in London."

"And you met our Duke, did you? Was your blood not blue enough for the likes of him?"

Hugh cringed. Was that how she viewed him? Even if there was truth in it, he had not thought it apparent to others.

"He was polite to me. But I was not one he would have considered for his duchess, 'tis true."

"Consider yourself most fortunate, then. I pity the poor girl who succumbs to the position."

"Perhaps he does not know any better," she replied in a reasonable tone.

"You are as naive as my sister. It suits you. I wish I had the luxury." Hugh could hear his boots on the stone as he continued to walk loudly up the stairs.

"This looks like an excellent signalling tower," Miss Craig stated.

Stupid girl! What game was she playing now? She was going to get herself killed! Hugh was hard-pressed not to run up the stairs and strangle her with his own hands to save Deuce the trouble.

"Signalling for what?" Deuce asked.

"Smuggling, of course. I thought everyone who lived on the coast was involved."

Hugh could just see the innocent look she was giving Deuce.

"Ah. That is what I hear."

"You know nothing of it?" Her voice held astonishment.

"Do you feel it in your blood? I also hear that can be the case." Amusement rippled through his tones.

"Perhaps I do. I confess to an unusual curiosity."

Deuce laughed. Hugh's skin crawled.

"I might know some people who know some people," he confessed.

"Do you think I could watch?" she asked. There was a disgusting amount of marvel in her tone.

"Hmm. I will see what can be arranged and send word to you."

"But how? I do not think my aunt would approve."

"Let me worry about her. I have my ways. The rain is letting up; we can probably continue, now."

Hugh slipped out of the door and away from their sight before they descended from the top of the tower. His mind was reeling. It was his fault Miss Craig was doing this—putting herself in harm's way

—but would she share the information with him? And how could he get a message to her?

∼

Maili was convinced her heart was going to explode inside her chest. When she arrived back at Brantley, her aunt was waiting, frantic with worry. It was late and dark, and there had been storms to slow their return.

Maili could not face her aunt's queries—her emotions were too raw. She pleaded fatigue after apologizing and reassuring her aunt, and left her uncle David to explain. She walked a few steps away from the parlour and then stopped. Her aunt and uncle David began to argue. Maili had already courted disaster—she had not intended things to go so far—and yet she could not resist the opportunity to find out more. She looked around and then stepped closer to try to hear what they were saying.

"How could you, David?"

"I'm sure I don't know what you mean," he drawled.

"I am not a fool! I have defended you and defended you, but this goes beyond the pale!" Aunt Brennan wailed hysterically.

"May I assume you refer to our lovely niece?"

"Stop being coy! You know very well what I mean; sending the children to an orphanage and telling us they were dead. Was it worth it?"

"Was it not rather chivalrous of me to allow them to live?" he retorted in a bored voice. Maili dug her nails into her palms in disgust.

"You will rot in hell for this!"

"And any number of other things," he agreed.

She made a sound of revulsion.

"I never told you they were dead, nor at an orphanage."

"Oh? What do you mean by that?"

"I was incapacitated, if you recall."

"Are you telling me you did not know?"

ELIZABETH JOHNS

Maili was sure her eyes could not grow any wider as she waited for the answer, but none came. There must have been some silent communication. She would be in peril if she were found, yet she could not walk away.

"What do you propose to do now?"

"I have not yet determined. She is quite a taking little thing, our niece."

"David..." Lady Brennan's warning voice sent a shiver of repulsion through Maili's frame.

"Maybe I will recruit her to work for me," he teased. "Oof!"

"Do be serious!" It sounded as though she had thrown a pillow at him.

"Why is that ridiculous? Smuggling is in her blood as much as it is in ours."

"Only by necessity." She seemed to speak through gritted teeth. "We should keep our voices down."

"I had best be going anyway. I have some business to arrange."

"Thank you for escorting her home safely. I cannot imagine what was in her head to go so far by herself."

"Can you not?" he asked, though he received no reply.

Maili heard the door begin to open. She ran up the stairs as fast as she could and still be quiet. She reached her room and leaned against the closed door, panting to catch her breath. So much had happened today and she could not sort through it all—she was unable to separate the facts from the emotions. She desperately wanted someone— other than her aunt or uncle—with whom to discuss this fantastical situation. The Duke of Cavenray immediately came to mind, then she dismissed it instantly. It was clear he and her uncle had some history, yet it was her uncle who was deemed to hold the dangerous reputation. But could she trust the Duke either? Especially if he had been the one to kill his father for interfering in his smuggling operation. Was everyone involved? She did not know who to trust.

It seemed there was something happening tonight, and she had to find a way to let the Duke know. She had promised. She would have to stay on amenable terms with both of them and hope that good prevailed in the end, and she did not risk everything in the meantime.

She began to pace her room. How was she to get word to him? He would not be expecting a note in the folly. Should she attempt to slip out and take it to him? That was too risky, especially after her adventure to Crossings—and she was so very tired. It had been an exhausting day, both physically and emotionally. Could Lilly be relied upon to keep quiet? She would have to take the risk. She sat and penned a quick note and rang for the maid.

"Lilly, can I trust you?" she asked in a secretive whisper.

"Of course, miss. What do you need?"

"I have a note I need delivered to Gracemere, post-haste. Can you get it there?"

The maid stood for a minute staring, wide-eyed, before answering. "I think I know a way. You leave it to me, miss."

"Thank you, Lilly. And no one must find out, do you understand?"

"Yes, miss, completely."

"Thank you. I am going to rest for a while. Can you tell my aunt I will not be down for supper and wake me when you are ready to go to bed?"

Lilly looked confused, but nodded. "Yes, miss."

CHAPTER 14

*E*mory burst into the study in a most uncharacteristic fashion. He was panting, clearly out of breath. His hands were balancing him against the doorframe.

Hugh looked up and waited.

"There's going to be a big run tonight, your Grace!"

"Indeed?"

"I overheard the news at the inn you sent me to."

"Any more details?"

"No. They were just drinking and talking before preparing to leave, when I heard. I came back as quickly as I could. You do not seem pleased." Emory pouted.

"You have done excellent work, Emory." Hugh attempted to placate the man. "I am just not surprised, that is all." He held up a letter which had been waiting for him when he had at last returned from stalking Miss Craig for the entire day.

"So you already knew?" the valet asked in shock.

Hugh inclined his head. "Do not to be disappointed. I do not consider your time wasted. If this had not arrived, then how else would we have known? Besides, you will be able to assist in identifying the culprits."

Emory thought about it for a moment then his chest puffed back out a bit. "I expect so," he comforted himself. He once again turned his attention toward the Duke.

"You are an abomination! What has happened to you?"

Hugh sighed loudly. "I have been on a wild goose chase all day." He waved his hand for Emory to sit. "I began the day intending to survey Sir David Douglas's land, Crossings. However, as I set out on Goliath, I saw a lady pass in front of me, galloping across my land as though the hounds of hell were after her."

"What lady would dare trespass upon Gracemere?" the valet asked in obvious offence.

"The guest of our neighbour, that is who," Hugh replied. "We became acquainted in London. So, naturally, I felt obliged to follow her. Her destination was Crossings, as I suspected."

"Why did you suspect?" the valet asked with a wrinkled brow.

"That is a very long story, Emory," Hugh said, resignation in his voice. "She is the niece of Sir David Douglas, affectionately known—as you are aware—to both of us as Deuce."

"But why follow her?"

"Because she has no sense and was putting herself in danger. She was thought to be dead. and Douglas apparently was responsible for sending her and her siblings to an orphanage. Douglas therefore did not know of her presence here. I thought her in danger."

"Is she? Was she?"

"It is difficult to say. Douglas appeared very sanguine about seeing her."

"He was there?" Emory asked, his face alight with anticipation.

"But of course. He invited her inside the house after sending her groom home."

The valet gasped theatrically and moved to sit on the edge of his seat.

"No, no, nothing so exciting. I do not know what happened inside the house, but I followed them back and a storm came upon us. They took refuge in the folly and I managed to overhear some of their conversation."

"Did you think he was going to kill her? Push her from the top?"

"That would have been rather bold of him, although I do believe him capable. It was rather dull, in actual fact. She did a convincing job of playing a silly young chit, which she very well may be; she asked him about smuggling and feigned a believable interest in it. She even asked if he could arrange for her to watch a run."

"No!"

"Yes, I am afraid so. Now, therefore, our job not only entails trying to see Douglas caught, but also to protect her."

"Why should we protect her?"

Hugh sent a scathing look towards Emory. "Because I order it so, Emory. It is the gentlemanly thing to do," he added, annoyed he sounded defensive.

"Yes, your Grace," the valet said demurely. "Do we need to prepare anything for tonight?"

"Something old and dark would be preferable."

Emory sniffed in offence that his Grace would think he owned any such thing—or that he would allow it.

"Borrow such attire if you must, but I would prefer not to be obvious amongst a gang of smugglers, if you understand me."

"I understand, your Grace. What time would your Grace desire to be readied?"

"I intend to have my supper as usual, followed by a nice, warm bath."

"Very good, your Grace. The valet bowed out of the room. Hugh chuckled to himself. He had stolen Emory's thunder and hurt his feelings. He would make it up to him later.

There was a knock on the door.

"Enter," he commanded.

"There is a message for you, your Grace." Walton shuffled into the room and handed the sealed letter to him.

Hugh opened it and began to scan Miss Craig's handwriting. She knew of the run that night. She had heard from her uncle's own mouth.

"Will there be any reply, your Grace?"

"No, Walton, you may go."

"Good girl," Hugh said to himself, tapping the letter against his hand. He had been uncertain whether Miss Craig would choose to share any more information with him. This was a good start, but would her loyalties lie with her uncle in the end?

~

Maili could scarce keep her eyes open long enough to climb into the bed. Once she was between the sheets, though, pictures filled her mind's eye. She began to see her father carrying her around on his shoulder, dancing in circles, and both of them giggling with uninhibited pleasure. But then, her Uncle David was there, and her papa was not happy any more. They began to argue over something she could not understand.

"There is something honourable for you out there, David. The church, the army, the law..."

"That is easy for you to say, when you had Crossings handed to you because of your birth," he snarled.

"I am sorry for something I cannot help, especially if this is what it has done to you," her father said sadly.

"Then do not begrudge me what I must do to survive."

"What do you mean, David? What have you planned? There are already those who suspect your involvement."

"Nothing you need worry about. I will not tell anyone I am your brother."

"I am not ashamed of you, David."

"That is priceless, coming from you, Nigel. You can take your perfect estate and perfect little family and rot." He stomped away, leaving her papa and her staring after him.

Maili felt someone shaking her shoulder. "What? Huh?" She struggled to open her eyes.

"You said to wake you when I went to bed, miss."

Maili sat straight up as she remembered what was going on. "Yes, thank you, Lilly. Was the message delivered?"

"Yes, it was, miss. Jemmy's grandpa is the butler there so he has an excuse to visit any time he chooses.

"That is a relief. Thank you again, Lilly."

"I am happy to help, miss. Do you need my assistance tonight?"

"No, you go on to bed." Maili shook her head. "I just want to watch."

"I done that once or twice," Lilly admitted. "Should I go with you?"

"I will not be alone," Maili responded with a reassuring smile.

"That's all right, then. Ring if you need me when you get back. I'll try to let you sleep as late as possible." The maid winked conspiratorially as she bobbed a curtsy and left the room.

Maili found she ached all over when she tried to get out of the bed. It had been months since she had ridden and she should have known better than to travel over twenty miles her first day back in the saddle! She never should have taken a nap in the first place; it was much harder to get up, now.

She pulled out her darkest dress and her oldest boots, hoping that would keep her hidden. To dull her white skin, she even put a little soot from the fireplace on her cheeks.

Grabbing her cloak, she opened her door quietly and checked the hallway before sneaking down the backstairs and out into the dark night.

There was a low mist hanging over the ground, creating an eerie aura of anticipation. Maili did not know where she should go, so she headed back to the boulder she had hidden behind before. Although it was difficult to see, she could hear the lapping waves of the sea nearby. The briny air was thick with the smell of salt and seaweed, and gulls' cries were still echoing overhead.

"Overhear, did you, my love?"

Maili about jumped out of her skin.

"Oh, Uncle David! You gave me such a fright. Yes, you and my aunt were not precisely quiet." For some reason she was shaking and having difficulty mastering her own voice.

"I thought you might have, but you should be a bit more cautious, running tame on the beach at night," he warned. "But since you are here, I might as well put you to use."

She perked up, nervous and excited at the same time. She did not want to do anything illegal, but how else was she to find out anything?

"What can I do?" she asked eagerly.

"With the fog, I need an extra lookout. I can put you up in the tower, though I doubt you will see much from there. I have my usual man watching to the south from the ground."

"Do you mean the tower at Gracemere?"

"Yes, the one we were in earlier today. It is simple—all you do is flash the lantern once if you see our ship—they will flash once first and you flash them back once, or you flash twice if you see the Revenue men."

"Once for a ship, twice for the Revenue men," she repeated to herself.

"Are you brave enough to go up there alone and wait? It can be some time."

"Of course." How frightening could it be?

"Good girl," he said as he tweaked her chin. "I'll fetch you a lantern."

He went into the hut and returned with a glass lantern containing a lit candle.

"This should last you long enough. Keep it hidden in your cloak, and only show it enough to light your way until necessary for signalling." He turned to leave. "When will I know it is over?" she asked.

"When you see the ship leave," he replied. It appeared simple enough.

She watched him walk away, the dream she had had earlier still on her mind. Was it a real memory? How could she know?

She turned and made her way to the folly, wondering if the Duke had received her message and what, if anything, he would do. Her mind was not yet clear about whom to trust. They could both be up to no good. It seemed certain her uncle was engaged in wrong-doing, yet she could not bring herself to loathe him as she probably ought. There were still many questions left unanswered and she wanted the chance to ask.

The heavy wooden door to the folly creaked open and she began the long, winding climb up the hundred or so stairs. It was unnerving in the dark, alone. The single taper provided very little light, and she wondered how a ship would see it, though she had seen it quite clearly from the beach the other night, when it was not foggy.

Every few steps she stopped and held the light up around her, certain someone was following her.

"Drat that Anne Radcliffe and my dreadful imagination," she muttered.

She hurried up the stairs as quickly as she could, trying not to slip on the frigid, wet stone. Even inside the tower it was cold and windy, and despite the high vantage point, she could see very little. Had she been sent up here to be kept out of the way? She frowned at the notion.

CHAPTER 15

*H*ugh was dressed all in black ready for the evening's events, and he had a day's growth of beard to help hide his face. He pulled his hat down low and stepped into the cold, misty evening. He had a pistol in his belt and a knife strapped on his arm. Hopefully, they would not be needed, but it was best to be prepared. He knew Miss Craig would be out there somewhere, but where? Had she cajoled Deuce into letting her help already?

He walked down to the beach in complete darkness. There was no moon at all tonight. He trod as cautiously and quietly as he could, but the rocks under his feet seemed to echo loudly. He hesitated when he reached the folly. He would have a better view of the beach from there, though he doubted he would see any ships because of the low fog. Would they still attempt to signal from out there? If the organization were down to him, he would move the signal to a lower point along the coast. The only problem with watching from the tower was, if Miss Craig was on the beach and in any danger he would not be able to go to her aid with any speed.

He stopped and, looking up, wondered if anyone was in the folly. First, he debated having a look. He opened the door cautiously, not wanting to give himself away in case one of the smugglers was already in there. Although he had every right to be on his own land, he did not know how they would react if surprised. In the darkness, his ears seemed sensitive to every noise. He tiptoed as quietly as he could on the steps, but then froze when he heard a voice. He strained to hear. Silence.

A faint light flashed ahead of him and he took a few steps, staying back against the cold stone wall. He was determined to have a glimpse of the smuggler.

The person seemed to be muttering to themselves. He could detect an occasional string of words but no reply. He continued creeping up the stairs until he reached the upper chamber, when he saw her familiar form. She was covering a lantern with the thick fabric of her cloak, though there was enough light for him to discern her features. She was looking out intently over the water and did not seem to notice his presence. He walked closer.

"Have you seen anything yet?" he asked in a hushed voice, directly behind her.

She jumped with fright, straight into him.

"Do not scream," he commanded as he caught her and tried to protect the lantern.

"You should not creep up on people like that!" She turned her head, managing to chide him without taking her eyes off the water.

"You should always be alert for predators."

She did eye him then. "Thank you for the reminder." Her voice dripped with derision.

It was going to require a great deal of effort to keep his hands from her, but he was determined he would do so.

"Have you seen any boats yet?"

"No, I arrived only a few moments before you."

"It could be early, yet. Did Douglas tell you anything about the operation?"

"No, and he was not surprised to see me, either."

"Did he try to deny his involvement?"

"Not at all. He and my aunt spoke somewhat loudly of it after we returned to the house. I overheard everything. I think she is involved, to some extent. I do not know how much, though she did not seem to condone the wrecking."

"I imagine her involvement is due to persuasion by her brother. I suppose it remains to be seen."

"I wonder what type of shipment they will be bringing in?"

"I only had word that it is coming in from India."

"India? You had word?" Her voice held surprise.

"Yes, I had written to the authorities in London and I only received a response today."

"Will there be a trap set for him, then?"

"I do not know. I have little knowledge of the depth of his operation. He has to have someone on the inside, providing him information. It will take some time to solve. Of course, there is always the chance that the Revenue officers will catch them."

She let out a gusty sigh.

"That sigh spoke a thousand words. Do you care to share them with me?"

"I do not know. On the one hand, it seems my uncle is a traitor or, at the very least, a criminal. On the other hand, there are many questions left unanswered that trouble me. He seems so charming, I would scarce believe he was involved if I had not heard the words from his very mouth!"

"He is extremely charismatic and convincing. He has always been thus."

"It is most vexing! This would be much easier if..."

"If he were an evil, mean, nasty ogre?" he finished for her.

"Yes!"

"That is why people like him are so elusive and deceive others with such ease. People refuse to believe them capable of such atrocities when they own a handsome face and a seductive smile."

"He was everything that was kind to me today," she explained.

"I will not ask what possessed you to go to Crossings alone," he growled.

"How did you know?" Her eyes were trying to examine him in the darkness. He could feel their perusal and her suspicion.

"I was going there myself, to investigate, when you flew past me on the dappled mare."

"So, you followed me?" Her eyes glared at him with disbelief.

"Naturally. You were with him, and on my land as well," he pointed out.

"I did not think you would mind," she said a little sheepishly."

"I did not say I minded, merely that I followed you," he drawled.

"I had not intended to go inside the estate. I only wanted to see where it was. My aunt had promised to take me to look around the house."

"But the groom persuaded you." It was not a question.

"Yes. I was never more shocked than when I saw my uncle walking towards me. He had told my aunt he was not staying there."

"I would not trust a word that comes from his mouth," Hugh warned.

"I think I see something," she whispered with excitement. "I wish I had a spy-glass!" she exclaimed.

He pulled one from his cape and began to scan the beach, then the water.

"Are you going to share?" she asked impatiently with her hands on her hips. By Jove, she was tempting him.

"That depends on the price you are willing to pay," he teased, deliberately lacing his voice with amusement.

"You rotten scoundrel," she said, stamping her foot.

"Perhaps," he answered with a chuckle. Relenting, he held the instrument out towards her.

She looked at it as though it was a hot iron and reluctantly took it, her curiosity getting the better of her.

"I see it!" she exclaimed like a small child.

She held up her lantern and flashed the light a single time.

A few moments later, there was a responsive signal from the ship.

"This is much more exciting than I thought it would be," she confided.

"As long as you are not caught. That would provide little enter-tainment."

She considered his statement. "I had not thought about being caught, but I suppose I am not out there handling the goods. Would I be hanged?"

"Not for being caught on my land, with me. There would be other repercussions, however. I hope this satisfies your curiosity about smuggling."

She took the glass and pointed it down towards the beach. Men came out from the fishing hut to assist with unloading the booty.

"Where do they put everything? The fishing hut is not very big," she asked, handing the glass back to him so he might look.

"I suspect there are tunnels," he replied.

"You have not seen them?"

"I saw no evidence of them when I first looked, but I was not searching for them. I think it worth investigating further." He held up the glass and scanned around. "Your uncle obviously has a sophisticated operation here."

She was squinting, trying to peer through the fog. It was difficult enough to see with the glass. It was some time before they saw any evidence of the boats. When lights began to flash from somewhere beyond the scene, several of the men began to wade out into the water.

Hugh assumed Lieutenant James had received his note, but he did not know if the officer intended to act tonight or not. Then he heard men shouting and saw the smugglers scrambling all over the beach.

"Trap! Trap! Get out of here!" men shouted.

"Are the Revenue men here? What do we do?" Maili asked.

"I assume that the run was intercepted somewhere down the coast and the Revenue men rode in on a dummy ship. The fog would have made it difficult to discern the difference until it was too late."

"Should we leave?"

"No, we should stay here until the coast is clear. You could be in harm's way if they decide to shoot each other."

He felt her body tense as if she had not considered they would fire upon one another.

The men looked like small animals scurrying around on the beach.

Officers began to emerge from the water, giving chase through the fog. A few men were caught and trussed up like livestock, while others did their best to get away. Enthralled, Hugh and Maili watched as much as they could see from the folly. It was as if they were watching a play. It was chaos.

"Quick, into the wall!" he commanded suddenly, pulling her with him. He took the lantern and found the latch and swung them into the small hole in the wall.

"What—?" she began to ask before he hushed her.

"Shh. I heard someone coming."

They were squeezed against each other in the small hole which had not been intended for two. If they were found...

Someone did come up to the landing of the tower in a rush of steps and made for the wall. It had not been so secret after all. Hugh held as tightly as he could to the latch in order to prevent the person from opening it.

The person, whom he presumed was Deuce, let out a string of curses. The voice was undoubtedly male. He felt Miss Craig cling to him more tightly and he prayed that this imbecile left soon, for he was finding it difficult to breathe as well as hold on to the latch with all his might.

Douglas tried the latch again and then they heard his steps retreating.

"Thank God," Miss Craig whispered. "Is it safe to go out?"

"Not yet." Much to his chagrin. "We want to be sure the coast is clear. I believe the officers will search for a while."

He shifted his weight to try to find a more comfortable position, but there was no way to keep from touching her. Several times he could hear shots fired in the distance, but she said nothing. She just leaned against him, almost as a child would his mother. He placed his arms around her, waiting for a protest, yet none came.

"Could we open the door for some air?" she suggested after some half hour had passed—a half hour where he had spent every ounce of his energy trying not to think about the luscious handful in his arms.

"An excellent notion. It should be safe now." He sprung the latch and breathed in deeply but Miss Craig did not move.

"I cannot feel my legs," she said shyly.

He picked her up and attempted to squeeze through the small door but the result was farcical and she fell on top of him.

"God above, I am only human," he muttered.

"What? Are you hurt?" she asked innocently.

"In a manner of speaking," he answered through gritted teeth. Why would the confounded woman not move off him? Did she not know what was good for her?

"Where is your pain?" she asked as she began to search with her hands.

He quickly grabbed them before disaster struck, but that only pulled her face closer to him. Despite his earlier resolution, he met his lips to hers and lost himself.

Throwing care to the wind, he reached up and brushed her lips. He peppered her face her eyelids, her ears, her neck, with soft kisses and he felt her sigh— hopefully it was from pleasure.

She looked up, and without hesitation, circled his neck with her arms. Her fingers gently combed through the hair on the back of his neck, stirring an awareness of his deep need and attraction to her. She opened her mouth slightly, and he took the opportunity to deepen the kiss—his own arms pulling her tightly to him. She tentatively kissed him back, her boldness only adding to his ardor.

Each of them caressed the other, both pulling the other closer, almost feverish in their need for each other—as if this could be their last kiss, a last opportunity to be together. Why, he could not think.

But think he must. He pulled back, his breath coming in heated pants.

"I should probably go, your Grace."

He heard the voice of reason say.

"Hugh. That would be wisest."

She rolled away to stand and he leapt up and assisted her.

"I will escort you back. I want to make certain no one is lurking.

She nodded in agreement.

They walked back in silence and did not encounter anyone on their way. Hugh would send Emory out to discover what had happened that night. He wanted a full report, but mostly he wanted to know if anyone had been caught.

In the meantime, he needed to think. She moved him like no other woman before. He missed her when she was not with him, and longed for more of her when she was with him. He realized with a start that his feelings for her had grown into a need to satisfy something deep within himself.

~

Maili groaned when the maid threw her curtains open the next morning. It had been five in the morning when she had finally tumbled into bed. Even then, she had not been able to fall asleep after the excitement of the night before.

"Close the curtains, Lilly, I need sleep," she grumbled.

"It is Sunday morning, miss. Did you forget?"

Maili groaned again.

"I let you sleep as late as I could."

"I think I will take a tray in my room this morning. Could you bring some coffee?" Maili asked with one eye open.

"Of course, miss. If you promise to tell me all about last night, I will fetch your tray," Lilly said with a cheeky grin as she closed the door.

Maili only wished she knew what *had* happened last night. There had been no sign of anything nefarious by the time she came down from the tower with the Duke. Her face blushed in remembrance of what she and the Duke had spent a good deal of time doing. He certainly had not acted as though he was disgusted by her. She tried to remain calm about it, reminding herself that he could merely have been taking advantage of what was before him, and also to guard her heart in the future.

There had been so much excitement here that she almost dreaded returning to Craig Castle. However, she did miss her family and would be glad to see them again. She had expected to receive a letter from her father by now. What could be taking so long?

Reluctantly, she climbed down from the bed and used the chamber pot before Lilly returned. The maid entered and set down her tray, the contents of which Maili began to sample while Lilly laid out her dress for the day.

"What time did you come in, miss?"

"Five of the clock," Maili answered wearily as she sipped her coffee.

"I heard they was caught by surprise."

Maili nodded, her mouth full of a roll. She swallowed. "How did you hear about it so soon?"

"No-one can speak of anything else below stairs, miss. And his lordship was called out to act as a magistrate. Did you see anything?"

"Very little, I am afraid. I was watching from the folly on the Duke of Cavenray's estate. There was heavy fog and I could only see partially, through a spy-glass."

The maid sat on the edge of the bench at the foot of the bed, eating up every word.

"Do you know who was caught? I stayed in the tower until the coast was clear."

"Not yet." The maid shook her head. "I expect we will know when we see who does not arrive at church this morning."

Maili doubted her uncle would have attended anyway, but she refrained from saying so. Or did everyone know he was the gang's master? She also doubted many minds would be on the sermon that day, but rather on the siege last night.

If only she had made plans to see the Duke again, she might find out more information than a maid could provide.

Lilly helped her dress and she ran downstairs in time to be handed into the carriage leaving for the church. She only prayed she had drunk enough coffee to keep her eyes open and not make a complete fool of herself. Her body betrayed her by emitting an unladylike yawn, which she hastily tried to hide behind her hand.

There was definitely a dull roar of chatter amongst the parishioners when they arrived. Maybe they hoped to discover some new information from the magistrate's wife, but Lady Brennan had been uncommonly quiet this morning.

Maili would not confess that she knew anything at all.

Mrs. Snodgrass hurried across the churchyard to greet them. She quickly said good morning and then pulled her friend away for a private talk. Maili did not know anyone else and just stood to the side, waiting and trying to overhear. She had become quite a shameless eavesdropper of late.

"All I know is three men were captured and taken to the gaol."

"You don't know who?" the vicar's wife asked with obvious disappointment.

"No. Brennan has not returned."

"For shame!" the woman exclaimed in a loud whisper. "It will be interesting to see which faces are absent this morning."

The bells rang and everyone hurried into the church. It was the shortest service Maili had ever experienced—not that she was not grateful on this particular occasion.

The vicar was clearly distracted by something and read through his notes as swiftly as he could draw breath.

When they were dismissed, no one seemed to think it odd. A large crowd remained in the churchyard to gossip.

"I will send word if I hear anything, and you do the same," Mrs. Snodgrass said to Lady Brennan, who was preparing to leave as soon as the carriage was brought around.

"Has something happened?" Maili asked after the door was closed upon them.

Her aunt paused before answering. "There was to be a smuggling run last night, but someone tipped off the authorities and men were caught. Some were shot and killed."

"Was my uncle involved?"

"I do not yet know," she whispered.

Maili felt sick at the possibility. She knew he had done bad things and he had hurt people, but she still did not wish him dead.

"Is there any hope for him if he lives?"

"I do not see how, Maili. If he had returned a changed man, it might have been possible. The people's memories are much longer in the country than they are in town, where scandals are common. Nonetheless, certain things are unforgivable anywhere."

Maili could only imagine what those things were, because her aunt said not another word.

CHAPTER 16

*M*aili spent the afternoon in the morning room, though it was dreary in there, with dark clouds outside obscuring the daylight. The house was strangely quiet and she had heard no more about the previous evening's events, or who had been taken prisoner. There was only one she knew, or about whom she cared what happened, but it was frustrating waiting for news, nevertheless. She decided to pen a letter to Gavin and Margaux, but it was difficult to know what to say. There were still so many unanswered questions, one being why had she not yet received word from them?

She told them of the lovely estate and how it overlooked the sea, and spoke of how kind and gracious her aunt was, but she hesitated to mention her uncle. After some deliberation, she decided to give them an account of her visit to Crossings, omitting her introduction to its owner.

There was very little else to say since she could not tell them what she had spent most of her time doing. Instead, she put down her pen and opted to rest on the longue for a little while, for she was still extremely sleepy from the previous night's exertions.

A knock disturbed her slumber and she attempted to tidy herself before calling: "Enter."

"A letter for you, miss," the butler said as he handed it to her.

"Today? How odd." She took the missive back to her chair and sat down. Sliding her finger under the wafer, she unfolded it. Another letter fell out from inside.

This letter was delivered to Gracemere by mistake. I believe my butler's eyes are failing. Meet in the folly at two if able.

~HD

That was all it said. She supposed it would not do for Hugh to write more. She opened the other letter, which was addressed in Gavin's handwriting, with anticipation. At least she knew why the letter was late.

My dearest Maili,

I trust this letter finds you enjoying a little holiday with your new aunt. I send this note from Alberfoyle, as promised. We have spent several days here, and are now on our way to Craig. I intend to leave Margaux there with Catriona, and then set out to bring you home within a few more days. Hopefully, that will allow you enough time with Lady Brennan. I know Margaux and I miss you, and wish you to be here with the bairn's arrival so close.

Now, to what you are probably scanning ahead to read – there were no records found of your or your siblings' existence at the orphanage. We searched and searched and came up empty-handed. No one seems to know what happened to them, but there are those in the village who remember you all. The house parents have now left but I have sent an enquiry on to them. There are almost entirely new folk working here since our time. I know this is disappointing, but hopefully we will be able to find Mr. and Mrs. Millbanks. Do not let down your guard, however. I believe your records were intentionally removed, or never there, but I cannot prove this, so do be careful.

Your doting Papa,
   Gavin

Maili blew out a breath with frustration. She had been counting on some resolution following Gavin's visit to Alberfoyle. How could files go missing so easily, with everybody being none the wiser? Had the caretakers decided the records were no longer necessary and disposed of them once she and her siblings had been given a home with Lord Craig? She could only hope that Mr. and Mrs. Millbanks would be found, and still remembered who had brought the Douglas children to the orphanage. It was hard not to feel hopeless. She was homesick; in all probability, her uncle was a murderer, a smuggler and a thief, who might be dead before she found out anything about their past. She was usually an optimist and generally felt that no one was ever beyond redemption, but if he was dead, it was too late. He was probably the only one who had the answers she sought.

She had met her aunt, and for that she was grateful, but it was almost worse knowing her uncle had very likely put her and her siblings into an institution and washed his hands of them.

Maili picked up her pen and decided to tell Gavin the whole.

My dear Papa,

I have just now received your letter. It had gone astray to another estate, and it was delivered to me a few minutes ago. I have met my Uncle David, who took over as baronet upon the death of our father. I had spoken to my aunt about him, and she confessed he was quite the scoundrel. She said he was forever getting into trouble as a youth, and he was forced to leave England in shame after killing a man in a duel. He is now returned to England, but only in secret, it seems. He is leading a gang of smugglers which is suspected of ship-wrecking—a most grievous offence. He claimed ignorance to placing my siblings and me in an orphanage, but I have not been able to ask many questions directly. Much of this is gathered from pieces of conver-sations. The strangest thing to me is that he did not seem surprised to see me at all. Otherwise, I am having a pleasant visit. Give my love to Mama and the children.

    Your loving daughter,
    Maili

She folded the note and sealed it with a wafer. She tucked it into her pocket and looked up at the clock on the mantel. It wanted a quarter before two. She would need to hurry to make it to the folly on time.

She was out of breath by the time she had walked briskly to the tower and then up the hundred stairs. She had not taken the time to check her appearance before she left. Why did she suddenly care what he thought of her? She needed to concentrate on the task at hand, since her papa would be coming for her within a fortnight at the very most. It was likely she would never see this Duke again, and she felt a pang of disappointment at that. If only she had known him like this in London.

~

Hugh had seen so much of Miss Craig in the darkness, that when she joined him at the top of the tower and pulled back her hood, showing her hair was loose and her cheeks in full bloom, he was ready to give the dukedom up to make her his. If only it were so simple. The time here with her had shown him there was more to her than the beautiful, but slightly vulgar, chit he had thought her to be in London. He had even noticed her idle chit-chat had greatly lessened. Perhaps it meant she was becoming more comfortable with him.

"Good afternoon, Miss Craig."

"Are we back to formalities, your Grace?" she asked boldly before showing him her dimple with a half smile.

"You have not told me your given name." He suddenly realized the omission.

"Maili," she said quietly, looking at him with those large, grey eyes.

"*Pearl*. It suits you," he said, holding her gaze for a moment before she looked away.

"Forgive my tardiness. I was finishing a letter to my father." She pulled it out of her pocket. "I wonder if you would mind franking it for me? I want to make sure my father receives it."

"Of course." He took the letter and put it in his coat. "I will see it is sent. Do you fear your mail will be tampered with?"

"I do not know what I believe at this point," she replied, beginning to pace around the chamber. "My heart and my mind do not agree on a great deal. I thought it best to be cautious."

"A wise move," he agreed.

"Why did you call me here? Do you have any information about last night? There are rumours that men are captured and some killed. We have no word about my uncle yet–or if we do, they are not being shared with me."

"Your uncle escaped," Hugh answered. He could tell she was relieved, by the emotion crossing her face.

"And the other men?"

"None of the local people were killed. Those men were from elsewhere and unrecognized."

"Thank goodness."

He saw her shoulders relax.

"It does not mean they are free from the hangman's noose."

"But I thought they had to be caught in the act, with goods, in order to be prosecuted?"

"It depends on witnesses and circumstances," Hugh explained. "If they were shooting at officers, that is enough."

"I would think the local people were not shooting. They were only doing my uncle's bidding. He is the mastermind."

"I agree he is the main target."

She grimaced but nodded her head anyway. It was clear she wanted an ideal in her mind for an uncle and most likely hoped to save him, yet at the same time, she was sensible about it.

"Thank you for telling me. Is there any further plan?"

Hugh should probably not tell her, though she seemed to be trustworthy. If she gave the plan away, then he would have his answer to that, but not have Deuce yet.

He wondered how long Deuce planned to continue this charade. He had to know the authorities were onto him.

"What are you thinking?" she asked.

"Forgive me, I was sorting the facts in my mind."

"And?" She was waiting with inquisitive eyes.

"I think your uncle knows this is his last stand. I do not think he intends to return and make this his home again." He stated the words as though he had received a prophesy.

"You think this is a final act of desperation?"

"I cannot say for certain, of course; it is merely a presentiment. He is not behaving like a man who would return to salvage his good name and become a country gentleman."

"He did say something of that nature when first we overheard him speaking with my aunt in here."

"Indeed, you are correct, I had forgotten. Then there must be some key to this ship. There has to be someone or something on it he thinks will save him."

"I cannot imagine what it could be," she said. Her forehead wrinkled adorably in consternation.

"I intend to find out. I just hope there is time. My valet has gone to see what he can discover from Lieutenant James."

"The Revenue Officer?"

"Yes. He knew of the run last night, so I expect he warned the ship off."

"Will they attempt to land here again? Was it even their destination?"

"It was, strange as it seems. Normally this is a sleepy smuggling town which goes unsuspected. It has therefore become an excellent route for trafficking items which would be difficult to conceal in more heavily patrolled areas. I do not think your uncle will make another attempt here now it has been found out."

"Thanks to you?"

"I suppose that is one way to look at it. He certainly will not have free rein here any longer. However, I strongly suspect he will not be able to change course with this ship at this late date. He has something riding on it and routes arranged, I am convinced."

"Why would he walk knowingly into a trap?"

"I surmise he will try to outwit us—do something risky."

"Such as make his manoeuvres during the day?"

"Yes, or take a hostage—something of that nature."

This was the reason he wanted—needed—to warn her. She would be ideal bait.

"Do you wish me to lure him?" she offered.

"No! That is the last thing I wish for. It is precisely why I asked you here today, to beg you to be more careful."

"That is the problem with smuggling, is it not? You never know who can be trusted. Even if people do not approve, they look the other way."

"Do you trust me, Maili?" he asked. He stepped closer and stroked his finger down her chin, then dropped his hand away.

"I want to," she said honestly.

He could not help but smile. "Fair enough. Have I ever done anything to make you think I am unworthy of it?"

"I suppose not."

"How very gracious of you. No doubt the verdict is still out on your uncle. However, you do know of his dangerous past. Yes?"

She nodded her head.

"So, I only beg you to be cautious. I would prefer you not be alone with him at the very least."

"Why does it matter to you, sir?" She looked up and searched his eyes.

He had walked straight into that. He inhaled deeply. "Should I not care? Knowing how dangerous your uncle is, should I allow you to play into his hands? I grant you he might have some conscience; he did allow you and your siblings to live."

"If that was his decision," she grumbled.

"However, we do not know for certain. Do forgive me, but I do care." He looked at her meaningfully—half willing her to understand and half willing her to not.

She looked away. He longed to take her in his arms again and show how he truly felt, but this was neither the time nor place, and he did not know how the situation with her uncle would end. He would do his best to protect her and see how the drama evolved. Being here, away from the *ton*, made him care less and less about doing his duty according to their rules. It was his life to live— his happiness.

The Titian-haired beauty was looking out over the sea, though it was too cloudy to see far. What he would not give to know her thoughts. He walked to stand next to her, overlooking the ledge, and could tell she was struggling with her emotions as she worried her lower lip. He placed his hand over hers and simply held it to give comfort. He knew she did not fully trust him, and he was not sure if she even liked him. She did respond to him.

"I do not know what I should do," she whispered.

"Nor can I tell you," he replied. "The best I can advise is to listen to your instinct, to your heart."

"Why must people be like this?"

"That is a question I cannot answer. The quest for power often begets evil."

"Says the man who was born to be a duke."

"Indeed," he muttered. She had a point, he conceded reluctantly. He had not thought she cared one way or the other for his title. Was that what the strain was between them after all?

"I ought to be grateful to him for one thing, at least," she said, still staring at the water.

Hugh turned her towards him and raised an eyebrow awaiting her answer.

"I could have been brought up by him. If he had not sent us to the orphanage, who knows what might have become of me, of us?"

"You never could have been like him, Maili. I cannot believe it of you."

CHAPTER 17

The Duke walked Maili back towards the divide in the pathway and said farewell. They had begun going their separate ways when a loud, cracking sound rent the air.

"What was that noise?" she turned back to ask. They looked at each other to see if the other knew what was happening, but the Duke appeared to have no more idea than she did.

"I think it came from the beach," the Duke said. They both hurried towards the water as fast as they could and were panting for breath when they reached it.

"Look! A ship has run aground on the rocks!" He pointed to where a ship had indeed run into some outcroppings of rugged boulders. It was difficult to see through the rainy mist that had begun to fall.

"Is there an alarm we should sound for help?" she asked.

"We are too far from the village. Run to the house and they can spread the word. Have them send for the physician and have Jemmy go and fetch my valet."

"What will you do?"

"I will try to see if anyone can be saved," he answered over his shoulder as he began to run again.

"Be careful," she called out to him.

She gazed at him long and hard before turning and going for help. An overwhelming feeling struck her. Something was about to happen and she should tell him that she did not despise him anymore. Did he even know how much she had loathed him? She wanted to apologize but there would be time later—she hoped.

Worrying as she sped towards the house, many different eventualities filled her head and she had to tell herself not to fret. In one, Deuce was killed. And in the other, Hugh was killed. When had she started thinking of him as Hugh and not the Duke? He certainly seemed miles away from the man she had thought him in London.

She ran into the kitchen and tried to relay the news to Cook, assuming the woman would be capable of spreading the word for help faster than she could herself. She passed on the Duke's instructions to Jemmy, before gathering as many supplies as she could think of from her years growing up with a physician for a father. Catriona and Seamus were much more suited to healing and had taken up their papa's profession. Maili did not have the gift nor the constitution for blood, but she was tough and she knew a few things. How could one not learn something with two physicians and a healer in the family? If only it could be enough to help today, she prayed.

Armed with blankets, bandages, water, soap, flint, laudanum, spirits and scissors, she charged back down to the beach, hoping that there would not be as big a disaster as she feared. Servants came running down the hill behind her with ropes and shovels.

The ship had begun to break apart by the time she made it back to the scene. People were screaming for help, and it looked like some of them were trying to swim towards the shore. The servants were tying ropes around themselves and wading out to meet some of those who were drifting on the tide. She looked around for Hugh, but could not see him anywhere. She held up her hand to shield the mist and squinted to see if he was one of those swimming, but she did not think so. Then she thought she detected a rowing boat from the north, and suspected it was he since it was coming from the direction of Gracemere. She began to sway back and forth with him as he heaved the oars back and forth, willing him to get there in time to save the poor sailors.

Part of the sloop began to break apart and she heard more cries and screams of desperation. She saw no sign of her Uncle David, and for that she was grateful as well. Dare she hope this was just an awful accident and not his intentional doing?

The fog seemed to be rising from the sea, and visibility became poorer. More people arrived to assist in the rescue, including the Revenue. They descended on horseback, guns drawn, as if they were prepared for a fight. Their leader quickly decided they needed to be closer to the carnage and shouted instructions before they rode away again to try for a closer vantage point to the vessel. It was eerie, Maili could hear more than she could see. The sounds seemed to carry through the cove and the fog.

She worried that if her uncle were there trying to raid the boat for goods, he would be caught. As the first sailor was finally hauled up onto the shore, Maili hastened to assist him and had little time to fret over what was happening out on the ship. She felt rather helpless and suddenly wished she knew what to do, other than try to keep the man dry. He already looked fatigued from the swim. She walked him a few feet further from the shore and then wrapped him in a blanket and gave him a sip of spirits to revive him.

"Thank'ee miss," he rasped.

"How many were on your crew?" Maili heard one of the servants call to him.

"Crew of twelve and four passengers," the man struggled to say. He did not look at all well. Could having to swim so far cause illness? She wished she knew.

She repeated what he had said to the servant, and looked out to sea, trying to count.

"I can count six heads in the water and there may be some on a row-boat," she told him.

She felt helpless as she watched the men labour to pull in the struggling swimmers. Even she could tell that they were beginning to tire and slow down. She had thought she would be more useful on the shore once the sailors were rescued, but now she was not certain everyone would be saved.

She only hesitated for an instant before she removed her boots and charged out into the water to help one figure she saw was too far from the rescuers. It was much colder then she had anticipated, and harder to walk against the waves pushing towards the shore past her heavy skirts. As the water reached her waist, she realized she was going to be indecent in her peach cotton day dress, but she could not watch while someone drowned if there was something she could do to prevent it. She was within a few feet of reaching one man. She saw his eyes filled with panic, but then his head began to bob up and down. He was losing the struggle.

"Wait! I am here!" she called to him. "Please fight! I am coming to help!"

She was too late; the man slipped under and did not come back up. Diving under the surface, she tried to search for him, but could not see through the haze, and the salt water burning her eyes. Out of necessity, she had to come up to the surface for air. *No, no, no, no, no,* she told herself. Refusing to give up, she dived back under a second time, swam forward a few feet and hit something. She grabbed onto it and struggled to pull the heavy weight up to the surface. It seemed like an eternity before she was able to catch another breath. She rotated the body over until his face was upwards, and began to swim with all her might towards the shore. Someone was there to help her pull him out, for which she was extremely grateful. Despite her own shallow breaths and trembling limbs, she forced herself to follow and began to beat on the man's back, hoping it would force the water out, but he did not even cough. Nothing was happening and she wanted to scream. She tried harder.

"It ain't no use, miss," she heard someone say, as a hand touched her shoulder. "You did your best. There are more we can help."

Maili knew he was right but she wanted to stay there and cry over the life she had failed to save. Looking up, she saw the other servants were still trying to help people and she forced herself to her feet.

"I am sorry," she whispered on a sob to the man. After saying a prayer for his soul, she hurried to help some of the other poor wretches who had been pulled from the water.

She bandaged a man's head and she wrapped others in blankets. A boat was being rowed towards the shore and more people had arrived to help. There were horses and a wagon near the track to the beach, but she could not have described much more of the scene. The rope brigade was still helping people wade out of the water to safety. Looking up, she noticed several small boats surrounding the wreck. *There must still be some men on the ship*, she thought.

She went to see if the first man who had been pulled out was any better. He seemed to have recovered enough that his colour was improved.

"Is there anyone missing?" she asked.

"I don't see the Cap'n or the secret passengers," he answered as he looked around.

"Secret passengers?"

He shrugged. "Sometimes they bring important people and we aren't to know who they are. 'Tis what we call 'em."

The cold chill was permeating through her sopping gown and she shivered as her teeth began to chatter. There was little time to think of her own comfort. She squinted hard to try to see what was happening, but it was too far away to make anything out clearly. Debris was washing on to the shore, mostly splintered wood, and the wrecked vessel had begun to sink. The bow was caught on the rocks, but the stern was drifting into the sea. To Maili's untrained eye, it looked too hopeless to try to save anyone else. How she wished she were closer, or had a boat to go and see for herself!

There was little else she could do for the moment, except await the fate of the remaining crew still to be saved. Two sailors had drowned so far, their bodies lying nearby covered, and the others who'd survived were huddled, shivering in their blankets—some coughing to try to clear the water they had swallowed and others were casting up their accounts.

Then, from the corner of her eye, she saw her aunt and uncle rushing to the scene. She must look a fright! She had been too concerned about everyone else to think of her own appearance.

"Maili!" her aunt cried when she saw her. She looked down at herself and realized she was, in fact, immodest. Her dress was of course wet and plastered to her like a second skin. Not quite as bad as being unclothed, but akin to wearing only a nightrail; it was a testament to the disaster that, as far as she was aware, no one else had noticed. Having hastily removed her own cloak, her aunt was trying to wrap it around her.

One of the men began to lose his stomach contents again and her aunt shrieked as they landed at Maili's feet and splashed her already ruined dress.

"You should leave, Aunt."

"And you should stay? I think not!" she protested.

"I have dealt with similar situations. My papa is a physician, as is Seamus."

"She is right, my lady, you should go." A man Maili had never seen before spoke from behind her. "Some of these men look like they have contagion. They will need to be quarantined for a while."

"Come, Annie," Lord Brennan said, trying to turn her back to the house. "There is no telling what they have brought in with them from the East."

"Very well. Come, Maili." She held out her hand.

"I am afraid she has been too exposed, my lady. She cannot return with you until she is declared clean," the stranger said.

"But she cannot be left with these... these ruffians!" Lord Brennan was continuing to back her away with him. "Can she not be quarantined in her room at Brantley?"

"She can help me tend to them. They are in no condition to threaten her, and I am afraid I will need her help. She seems to have some knowledge of nursing, by the look of things here."

129

It must be a surgeon who was speaking. Maili nodded. She did have a little experience, mostly from watching. She was willing to try.

"Who will chaperone her? And where will you take them?" her aunt asked, trying to stop her husband's forward progress. "She is a lady!"

The man looked as though he was thinking. "The church is the only place large enough."

"Gracemere is empty," Lord Brennan suggested. "I trust Mrs. Sizemore to look after Maili, and his Grace would not object, I am sure." His tone of voice indicated he would brook no arguments from her aunt.

"Keep me informed, Mr. Jarrell. I will, of course, send over a portmanteau with Miss Craig's possessions and anything else that is needed."

Lady Brennan gave Maili a look of apology before being led away by her uncle.

"But you would expose the servants there?" Maili asked the surgeon with surprise.

"There are fewer there than anywhere else," he replied.

Maili knew he was right, but how could they just take over the Duke's residence without permission from anyone? Perhaps her uncle as the magistrate had that power, but how could she warn the Duke?

She looked at the ill sailors sitting in front of her and knew they were in for a long night—or fortnight.

∼

Hugh assessed the damage to the ship as best he could from the beach and quickly decided he would be of more use if he had a boat. He ran to his own boathouse and unhitched the ropes before he began rowing the small craft out towards the shipwreck. Some of the sailors had already begun to swim towards the shore and looked as though they would reach it safely. Hopefully, Miss Craig would be able to gather enough servants to help them.

He kept going towards the ship, wondering what it was that Deuce and his gang were interested in. As he grew closer, he noticed a hive of activity on the other side of the broken vessel. There were many boats there; some men were gathering up barrels and other goods which were floating to the surface. There seemed to be little regard for the sailors who were trying to survive in the water. Hugh began to boil with anger. He supposed there was one good thing—they had not tried to murder the crew—yet. He had heard of such horrors where the wreckers had killed any survivors.

The gang seemed to pay him no mind as he grew close, so intent they were on their task. What could be in this wreckage that was worth it to Deuce? He still had seen no sign of him.

The bow of the ship had run aground on some rocks and the hull was speedily taking on water. As he pulled alongside the ship, shots begin to descend all around him from high up on a ridge above the shore. The Revenue had arrived and he was about to be caught in the middle of it.

"Help me!" Someone called to him, but he was afraid to look up to see who for fear of being hit. If only he had a way to signal to Lieutenant James.

"Over here!" someone said again, trying to get his attention. He tried to pull behind the boat for protection, and finally saw who it was: the devil himself.

"Please help me get out of here," Deuce pleaded. Then he realized who he was speaking to. "Your Grace. I never thought to see your face again."

"And I never thought you would be asking me for help."

"I would not ask if it were for me. There is a passenger who needs saving." Deuce carefully pulled a female forward so that Hugh could see he was telling the truth. But who was the lady, and why was Deuce risking his neck to save her?

A shot ricocheted off the mast and all of them ducked. "Please! I can explain later but you must help me protect her now."

"Are there any other passengers left on board?" Hugh asked.

"None who are alive. All of the living have swum towards the shore."

Hugh did not like to make decisions in haste, but it was clear they would all be killed by the Revenue if they remained here.

"Very well. Get in and row towards Gracemere. I will protect your lady for now." He was not about to risk being shot himself. If Deuce wanted to get away, he could row the boat.

Unfortunately, the lady was not well. Something was amiss. Either she had swooned from the shock of the wreck, she had been hurt, or she was ill. Hugh could not say which, but Deuce had to hand her limp body to him, which was a precarious proposition, what with Revenue officers shooting at them and trying to maintain his balance in the small boat.

He laid the lady down in the bottom of the craft and covered her with his body to protect her from the gunfire. She was small and frail, and did not look to be much older than Miss Craig. What in the world could be going on here? Deuce climbed into the boat and Hugh ordered him to row.

"As you wish, your Grace," he said mockingly.

Hugh glanced up as he felt the row-boat gliding away from the wreck. The stern was beginning to sink into the sea. There were still Revenue officers on the shore shooting, but none were having much success from land. The smugglers had simply moved to hide behind the wreckage and continued their looting.

Why had the Revenue not come by boat as they had before? Perhaps they had had no more warning than he had had. Now, what the devil was he supposed to do with Deuce and this lady? Hugh did not like to think of Deuce being charitable, but it seemed saving this female had come before searching for gold. Perhaps he did have a heart after all.

Speaking of ladies, he hoped Miss Craig was faring well on shore. There was a crowd of people there now, he could just make them out; some were helping the swimmers and others were piling up the debris, barrels and trunks beginning to wash ashore. There was a wagon there and some horses, so he assumed she was safe. He could not make Miss Craig out from this distance, which was odd. He would have thought she would stand out amongst men. And where could Emory be?

He watched as Deuce began to tire from the exertion of rowing. He was happy enough to share the burden after expending the effort the first time. He was in this position because of Deuce, and it was not much further to his dock. They were not being chased, so far as he could tell.

CHAPTER 18

$\mathcal{M}$aili watched as her aunt and uncle left her in the midst of this mess. She was quite certain her parents would not approve, and felt rather abandoned. However, she was resilient and these poor souls needed help. She gave a mental shrug and looked around to see where she could be useful. She certainly had not realized these men were ill; she had thought it all a result of their harrowing ordeal in the water.

They did not look well, but she had no notion of what ailment they might have. She was quite sure she looked as ragged as they. Had someone not mentioned they had come from the East? She had heard of some horrible diseases mariners could carry with them on board during family discussions. Since she was never ill, she did not worry too much about the risk to herself and set to assisting them.

The men were beginning to be loaded into the back of the wagon. She counted eight in total who still lived, and saw the others' bodies still lying covered on the beach.

"Do you wish to ride, miss?" one of the servants asked her.

"I would prefer to walk, thank you. I can cut across the back gardens and warn the household. I know the way."

"Very well, miss."

Maili gathered what remained of her supplies. She looked one last time at the remains of the wreck. It was hard to comprehend. Everything had happened so quickly, and she still had seen no sign of her uncle and did not know what had become of the Duke. He would certainly receive a big surprise, with all of the other passengers to be quarantined at Gracemere. Was she expected to nurse eight ill men alone? What madness had overtaken this surgeon and her uncle?

She walked, her arms full, trudging wearily up the hill, feeling exhausted and wanting to cry to let her emotion out. It was not every day someone died in front of her.

"This is no time for hysterics," she told herself. Her respect for her papa and siblings was already great, but now she understood the magnitude of what it took to give healing. "Please let me know what to do," she prayed as she walked.

She was calmer by the time she reached the house. She went to the kitchen door and knocked. There was no sign of the wagon having arrived, so she hoped she was in time to prepare the household.

Since no one answered her knock, she cautiously opened the door and looked in.

"Is anyone here?"

"What's that?" She heard a woman's voice ask.

"I am Miss Craig, Lord and Lady Brennan's niece. There was a dreadful wreck down on the shore."

"Yes, Jemmy came to fetch Emory, his Grace's valet. You look a fright, miss, if you'll excuse me saying so. Is everything all right?"

"No, I am afraid not." She was grateful she had her aunt's cloak or she would really scare the cook. "There are eight passengers who lived, but the doctor determined they were ill and needed to be quarantined."

"Oh, the poor souls!"

"No one knows his Grace is in residence, and the doctor volunteered Gracemere."

"Did he now? And who does he expect to be nursing them?" she asked, indignant.

"Me, I gather."

135

"His Grace will not be pleased one bit! A gently bred lady, cleaning up after a nasty bunch of sailors? No, no."

"My papa is a physician. I know much of what should happen."

"It does not make it right or proper. Does your aunt know of this?"

"She objected, but my uncle and the surgeon overruled her."

"Well, I never!" The woman was clearly offended more than Maili was.

"I had been helping the sailors and the surgeon considered me exposed. I came because I had to warn his Grace. Is he yet returned?"

"Do you know him, then?" The woman eyed her with a warm smile.

Maili nodded.

"I have not seen him. We do need to tell him. Let me think. Perhaps we could bring down the cots from the servants' quarters and set up a sick room in the saloon. It is on the side of the house closest to the privy and well, and is furthest removed from the rest of the rooms."

"I will find Watson and Mrs. Sizemore. The sick are on their way already, you say?"

"Yes, I expect they are not long behind me."

The cook shook her head and scurried about, muttering under her breath.

"Should I put some water on to boil, or fetch some blankets?" Maili asked.

"I suppose we should. I need Jemmy here to do the fetching for me. Do you think your aunt would mind if I kept him here? He is still in the stables admiring his Grace's stallion. I forbade him to go to the beach."

"I would not think so. He can explain after things have settled down."

Cook hurried off to find Mrs. Sizemore and Watson, and Maili set some water on the fire. When they came into the kitchen, she explained and they all went in different directions to begin preparations for the impending arrivals.

"Now, you stay away, you hear," she ordered Maili in a motherly way. "Let me deal with this. You watch for his Grace and warn him."

Maili wondered where the Duke could be. She gazed towards the sea, assuming he was out there somewhere.

"Please do not be harmed!" she whispered prayerfully as she watched and waited.

The wagon arrived and the servants went out to help the sailors into the house. She kept her distance as she had been told. She hoped none of them were carrying contagion, and wondered how long the surgeon planned to hold them all here. It could be weeks. Her heart sank. She desperately longed for home and her parents.

$\sim$

Once they were out of harm's way, Hugh sat up and helped Deuce into dock.

He was afraid to ask who the lady was, and what his adversary intended to do with her. He could not believe she was a complete stranger.

They tied the boat to a post and he climbed out ahead and helped Deuce to lift her.

"Bring her to the house," he told him. "I will send for the doctor and you can explain."

They were halfway up the hill when he saw Miss Craig running towards him, looking like a dirty, wet, urchin. She stopped in her tracks when she saw Deuce and his burden.

"What has happened? Is she dead?"

"She appears to be alive, but ill. Your uncle will have to fill in the details, as I am quite unaware of them myself," the Duke said curtly.

They began to walk again. "Wait!" Miss Craig objected.

"I would prefer not to, she is becoming quite heavy after my exertions," Deuce admitted with a wry smile.

"They have brought the sailors here. They all have the contagion, the surgeon said. He ordered them here and into quarantine. He believes the house to be empty."

Both men let out a string of curses.

"Thank you for coming to warn me," Hugh said to her. "Where have they put them?"

"They were making a sick room in the saloon. They have only just arrived and are still moving them in."

"We can go in through the south entrance," Hugh directed. "It leads to the private apartments." He began to lead the way and Miss Craig followed.

"I have been ordered to remain here, as well," she said as they walked.

"Ordered? By whom?" he demanded with considerable irritation. He held open a door for them to pass through and indicated a staircase.

"The surgeon felt I was exposed since I was assisting the sailors, and my uncle agreed."

"That surprises me not one bit," Deuce chimed in. "Brennan does not appreciate being inconvenienced."

"And your aunt threw you to the wolves?" Hugh asked, not bothering to mask his disbelief.

"There was little she could do," Miss Craig answered meekly. Hugh decided to cease harping on it. If it were found out he was in residence, everything would change. He strongly suspected her parents would not approve of the way Lord Brennan was looking after his niece. He would do his best to see no harm came to her.

"You may place the lady in here," he told Deuce as he held open the door to a large bedroom, which was decorated in hues of gold and yellow with floral-papered walls. "I will have my valet send for the surgeon, whose judgement is questionable if he is not presently attending our guests."

"Thank you," Deuce said, appearing grateful.

Hugh inclined his head. He did not know if the man was welcome yet or not. He certainly did not trust him.

"I will help her out of her wet clothes," Miss Craig said, taking over. "Fetch me some water and ice, if there is any." She removed her hand from the lady's forehead and looked to both of them to explain. "She has a very high fever. I do not know what is wrong, but I will help her the best I can."

Hugh and Deuce went into the hallway while Miss Craig removed the woman's wet clothing. Hugh wanted to soak in a long, hot bath, but luxuries did not seem to be in his future for at least the next fort-night. They went down the back staircase to the kitchen to see if any help was to be had, but no one was about. It was likely they were all assisting with the arrival of the sick.

Where was Emory when he needed him?

"The ice house is near the gamekeeper's cottage," Hugh told Deuce, who hurried off for the ice, and Hugh debated whether or not to reveal his presence to the surgeon. He certainly wanted to give the doctor a piece of his mind.

Finally, his wayward valet came bursting into the kitchen. "Your Grace! I have been to the ends of the earth searching for you!"

"I hope it was a delightful trip, and as you can see, I am here. Now do keep your voice down. We have some unexpected guests and I do not wish to be made known to them just yet."

"Who?" Emory looked stupefied.

"The sailors from the downed vessel were ill, and our good surgeon decided to quarantine them here since the house is believed to be unoccupied."

"He brought contagion here?" Emory's voice was just shy of a shriek.

"If you have a fit of the vapours, Emory, I am leaving you here. I have no time to search for smelling salts." Why did he put up with the man? "There is also a lady passenger upstairs in the yellow bedroom, being administered to by Miss Craig. Would you fetch the surgeon from the saloon, if he is there, and have him attend to her? I will remain out of notice."

Emory was clearly attempting to assimilate what was going on, and on this occasion words failed him, for which Hugh was thankful. The valet gave a quick bow and walked off to the saloon.

Hugh breathed a small sigh of relief and wondered if anything could have been done to prevent this disaster.

He walked through the servant's passage to the saloon to try to determine what was happening in the sickroom, and just what level of mayhem he should expect. He cracked open the door to have a look. Cots were set up about the room, eight in total. The surgeon was checking each of the men, and Hugh's cook, housekeeper and butler were cleaning and fetching things as directed.

"Do you know what is wrong, Mr. Jarrell?" Cook was asking.

"I cannot yet be certain, but it appears to be typhoid fever."

"Isn't that deadly?"

"It certainly can be," he replied.

"But I have never had it. Will we not all catch it?"

"That is unlikely. They were probably subject to a miasma on the ship—a noxious vapour—and came here with the disease."

"Then why must they be quarantined?" Cook asked with her hands on her hips.

"Because I cannot be certain at this point," Jarrell replied without a blink, clearly not willing to be questioned by a servant. "If it is typhoid, I expect there to be high fevers, severe aching of the head, and bilious stomach complaints. The course is much cleaner than cholera, so be thankful for that."

Hugh wanted to strangle the man for bringing this upon his household and threatening innocent lives, but the decision was made, and to move them now would only risk more people. He heard a knock on the door to the saloon, and Watson went to open it. There his valet stood, behind the door, unwilling to come in. The patients were shivering, some were coughing, and Emory had a severe aversion to illness.

"Sir, we have another person upstairs who is unwell. She was a passenger on the ship. She is in the yellow bedroom, if you could also look at her before you leave."

"Another one? How many more are there?"

"None to my knowledge," Emory explained. "She was brought in on a row-boat."

"Very well. I will go and see her." He turned to Cook. "Try to keep them cool and see if you can feed them barley water. There is little else to do for them. I do not know how long they have been ill, but the course takes about three weeks to subside—if they live."

Three weeks? Hugh groaned. This was not at all going as planned.

CHAPTER 19

A man Maili had not before seen showed the surgeon into the room, but did not stay. By this time, she had changed the young lady out of her wet gown and had given her a cold sponge bath. The woman's clothing was well-made, but there was little else to give clues to her identity. She seemed to be sleeping more peacefully now.

"Good evening, sir," Maili said to the surgeon, though she was not inclined to like his manner.

"Hmm, yes. I see you have removed her wet clothing. Excellent," he said as he surveyed the situation.

"She has a high fever, so I am bathing her in cold water. I have sent for some ice."

He began to look the lady over and noticed a rash on her chest. "It seems my diagnosis of typhoid was correct. She has the rash."

"Ship fever," Maili said quietly.

"Ship, gaol, camp, putrid, spotted fever—take your pick."

"Will they die?" she asked.

"I suspect some will. When added to the ordeal of a wreck and harrowing swim to safety, it will be too much for many of them to overcome."

"Two severe blows, the poor souls. Is there any quinine to reduce the fever?" she enquired, knowing it was the likely medicine her papa would have tried.

"What does a young lady know of quinine?"

"My papa is a physician," she explained.

"Indeed? Calomel will suffice for this," He said dismissively and pulled a small bottle out of his bag. "Five drops three times a day. Keep her hydrated as best you may. Many die from lack of water."

She nodded. She knew it well. Many illnesses wiped out villages because of fluid loss.

"You may send for me if she worsens, though there is little else to do for this. It is in the Lord's hands now." He shut his bag with a snap and left.

"Be that as it may, I intend to see you live, Miss...whomever you are... I would appreciate your full cooperation."

"You are so very much like your mother," her uncle startled her by saying. She had not heard him come into the room. "She was very determined in everything."

"I shall consider that a compliment."

"How is the lady?"

"The surgeon says it is typhoid. He says there is nothing to do but keep her fever down and feed her barley water."

"'Tis their remedy for every ailment."

"Do you know who she is?" Maili looked at him with suspicion.

"A fortunate lady to be alive. The other passengers and the Captain did not survive."

Maili felt sick herself when she heard this. If the Duke was correct, her uncle David had caused this.

"Why were you there?" she blurted out before she had a chance to think better of it. "Were you part of this gang I have heard about—a gang they say causes these wrecks intentionally, in order to plunder them?" She gazed at him hard, an unflinching stare.

"Have you already been poisoned against me?" His grey eyes studied hers.

"It is a simple answer, Uncle. Yes or no." She looked away. She could not bear to look at him any longer. At first, she did not think he would answer.

"No. I did not wreck this ship."

She whirled back to face him in astonishment.

"'Tis not the answer you expected. In time, I hope to improve your opinion of me."

"I would like that, very much," she said honestly. "It still does not explain why you were there. Did you not admit to smuggling?"

"Anyone around here is involved in smuggling, one way or another. Most laces and silks which your London modiste make your gowns from are smuggled goods."

"I had not thought of it in such a way," she confessed.

"Many choose not to think on it. To answer your question, I do not intentionally cause ships to be wrecked and innocent people killed," he answered as he stepped close to the girl and smoothed her hair back from her brow.

"I am glad to hear it. Do you know who does?"

"That is a very dangerous question, dear Maili. One you would best not ever voice again." His tone was warning enough to chill her to the bone.

The patient began to shake violently and groan as though in pain. Maili hurried back to her side.

"What is wrong?" he asked. He sounded genuinely worried.

"The fever, I suspect. The surgeon said it could last a few weeks." Maili began to dip cloths in the iced water and place them all over the woman. "She does not look so very old. I wonder if her family perished."

"I must leave to attend to another matter, Maili. Will you look after her?"

"Of course. I have nowhere else to go, after all."

He smiled at her, and turned to leave. She had a difficult time believing all her aunt had said of him. "Uncle David?"

"Yes?"

"Does she mean something to you, this lady?"

He sighed. "She means the difference between life and death to me."

She pondered that statement for several hours after he had left. What could he mean?

~

Hugh paced the study, wondering what his best course of action was. Deuce, whom he suspected to be the cause of the horrible catastrophe, was in his house at this very moment. Miss Craig, whom had come to possess too many of his rational and irrational waking moments, was also under his roof for an indefinite amount of time, and unchaperoned according to the rules of polite society. All the farce lacked was for his mother to arrive! Heaven forbid. *Forget you even had the thought!* he told himself.

Now, he not only had to worry his head over what Deuce was about, he had to consider the possibility of a contagion affecting his household, himself, Miss Craig...it was unthinkable. He was very tempted to carry her away, come what may. It was not an unpleasant thought.

A moment later there was a knock on the study door.

"Enter," he replied.

"Cavenray," Deuce said as he walked over the threshold.

"Sir David, I conjecture?" The man inclined his head. "Do come in."

"I believe we can dispense with the formalities. I appreciate your assistance today," Deuce said casually.

"I do believe I deserve at least some measure of explanation," Hugh said tersely.

"You sound like my niece."

Hugh's eyebrows raised in question.

"She is very direct, which I rather respect. She wanted to know if I had ordered the gang to wreck the ship."

"And what was your answer?"

"The same as it is to you. No, I did not order the wrecking of the ship, nor the other one two weeks past, nor any of the ones when I was here before."

"Although it would appear you have garnered quite the reputation for it."

"Which was the intended outcome," Deuce replied.

"With you as the scapegoat?" Hugh asked, eyebrows raised in disbelief.

Deuce gave a slight nod of acknowledgement.

"Do you intend to expose the man behind all of this? Why was he silent for the time you were away?"

"I pray this situation works in my favour. If all goes as planned, my name will be cleared."

"Indeed?"

"I know it may be hard for you to believe from our past, but on occasion, I can be charitable."

"So, you do not deny a history of smuggling?"

"I do not deny it, though I imagine my part was much smaller than I have been given credit for."

At least the man seemed to be candid. Hugh appreciated as much.

"Where have you spent your exile, if I may be so bold?"

"The West Indies. It became imperative that I leave."

"And what brought you back now?"

"The chance to clear my name and return home."

"Who is the lady you have brought with you? You know who she is, do you not? She was the treasure you sought on that ship."

"You always were very astute. No one else was ever able to see through my scheme at Cambridge."

Hugh remained silent.

Deuce stood up and thrust his hands into his pockets and began to pace the room. Hugh continued to wait. It appeared a confession was forthcoming.

"The lady is your half-sister. I took her away to protect her."

That was the last possible thing Hugh would have ever expected to come from Deuce's mouth. He was completely astonished.

"I beg your pardon?" He had a sister he had never heard a word about in his life? There had been nothing in his father's Will, he was certain.

"You heard me correctly. She is your father's love-child."

The confusion must have been written across Hugh's face.

"Your father loved to come here," Deuce said.

"Yes. But…" Suddenly, many things became clear. There were little things he could recall; his father had loved his mistress. Perhaps there could be a child, but Hugh did not know who the mother was.

"Why ever was there a need to take her away? I cannot believe my father would have harmed her."

"This is where the story grows dangerous to everyone involved. The less you know at this point, the safer."

"Oh, no, you do not drop this in my lap and then walk away." Hugh stood and strode towards Deuce.

That man held up his hand as if to ward him off. "It is not that I do not intend to tell you. The priority for now is keeping her protected and safe. Until she is well, I cannot do that if her presence is known. I must take myself away for a time. I trust my niece is more capable than the surgeon to care for her."

"You would risk Miss Craig's life for my half-sisters?"

"Of course not, but she already placed herself in that position. It is too late to dispute it now."

Hugh knew the man was right, the dastard.

"You care for her," Deuce remarked. It was not a question.

"And what is my half-sister to you? Why have you done all of this for her?" Hugh asked warily.

"All of these things cannot be answered simply. I know you do not trust me, but it will have to do."

"Does this sister of mine have a name?"

"Letitia—Letty."

"Letty," Hugh repeated, still trying to absorb his new family member's existence. "Where will you go? How will I communicate with you?"

"I cannot remain here because that becomes a threat to her. I care little for what happens to me. I know you will take care of her."

This was nothing like the man Hugh knew decades ago. He could scarce believe the honourable words coming from his mouth.

"You may leave me a note in the tower as you would have with Miss Craig." Deuce gave him a knowing look.

"How?"

"A man never reveals his secrets. I do expect an invitation to the wedding."

With that, the man left quietly, while Hugh remained behind stewing over everything Deuce had said.

CHAPTER 20

*M*aili jerked awake and saw the Duke standing there, looking at the lady patient. Night had fallen and she must have fallen asleep from exhaustion.

"I did not mean to disturb you. I know you need some rest," he said softly.

"I did not realize I fell sleep," she replied, wondering how long he had been there, and if she had been drooling, or—heaven forbid—snoring. She sat up and tried to tidy herself, but there was little point as she was still wearing the ruined gown from earlier, and her hair would be frizzed from being wet and uncombed.

The Duke hardly seemed to notice her, however; he was staring at the lady.

"Do you know her?"

He shook his head and whispered, "No."

He seemed disturbed, but Maili did not know what to say.

"How is she?" he asked.

"No worse than before. I have been keeping her fever down with the ice. I did notice some pink spots on her chest, which would confirm the doctor's suspicions of typhoid fever."

The Duke nodded yet looked distracted.

"Is everything all right?" she asked tentatively.

He furrowed his brow and bit his lower lip. She had never seen him look so vulnerable or unnerved. Despite her inner warnings, she walked over and reached out her hand to him.

"Your uncle says she is my half-sister," he whispered.

Maili had no words to offer, she could not know his feelings. She squeezed his hand in sympathy and he gripped it firmly, as though grasping for something tangible.

"Did he tell you her name? Or how she came to be here?"

"Letty. He says he had to bring her here to keep her safe. He refused to tell me more for now, but asked me to protect her."

Maili felt enraged. "He sends us to an orphanage, and he brings her here from far away? Why is he playing God with so many lives?" she asked bitterly.

"He led me to believe there is someone else who is still a threat. He would say no more. All we can do for the present is trust him."

"I want to. I need to know there is a reason for this madness! I do not want to believe he is evil enough to change our lives so grievously at his own whim."

"Maili, there are such people. Try not make much of it until this this business is resolved. And it will be. I mean to see the matter to a conclusion and justice served." His voice held a quiet menace.

"It seems we have little choice in the matter," she retorted.

He put his arm around her and pulled her close. "Would you care to bathe? It occurs to me you are still wearing the dress you had on when we attended the wreck."

"I am atrocious." It was an extremely inadequate word to describe her appearance.

"No, never that. Was it a ghastly ordeal?" Leading her to the bench at the end of the bed, he sat down next to her, never letting go of her hand. He turned to look at her.

Maili did not want to relive that afternoon. She could only nod her head. He must have seen the anguish on her face and he pulled her close to him. She did not want to cry, but her body shook with grief.

"There was a man who died because I could not reach him fast enough. My skirts held me back in the water. I watched the look on his face as he took his last breath," she recalled the horror.

The Duke inhaled deeply. She could feel his chest rise and fall. It was comforting to feel his arms around her, yet he must think her silly. "You poor girl. I never imagined you would try to rescue the sailors yourself."

"I saw him struggling and unable to reach the rope line. I do not think the servants could swim. They did the best they could."

"We all did. There were several who I could not save, either."

"And to think this was done on purpose! How could anyone be so evil?"

"They will be punished, you have my word."

She wanted to believe him. "Now we must nurse these poor souls who were unfortunate enough to have been sick. I am exhausted from swimming, and I was not unwell."

"Yes, it was a cruel blow, to be sure."

"I wonder how the sailors are faring?"

"Mrs. Sizemore said one of them has already passed away. The others are perhaps worse than Letty. Many of them are coughing."

"They probably took water into their lungs. It will be a miracle if any of them survive."

"At least they have a chance, now. I will have a bath readied for you, and I will stay with her so you may rest. My poor valet, though he is no good in the sick room, he is a gem otherwise. He will assist you as much as he may."

"Thank you. I am very sorry this has happened."

"I only hope, when this is over, that you will thank me," he said with a wry look. "We have a very long way to go yet."

Hugh pulled an armchair next to Letty's bed, expecting a long night. It still did not seem real to have a half-sister. Who could her mother be? He wondered how long it would take her to wake up, or indeed if she ever would. He wanted to see her eyes, her personality, her soul. He

151

already felt cheated, and to think he could lose her again when he had just found her! He had never thought to be grateful to Deuce Douglas for anything. Although, would Deuce have brought Letty to him had the situation been otherwise? Or would he have tried to extort money from him in exchange for his sister? He did not want to know. Many of his kind would not think twice about a bastard sibling, but he had never had a sister and it was a link to his father. His sire would expect him to take care of her. A love-child, Deuce had called her. There had certainly been no love between his parents.

He looked more closely at Letty. She must be at least five-and-twenty years or so. She was certainly not a child. Her hair was black, like his and their father's, and he fully expected to see his dark blue eyes gaze back at him when those lids opened; he prayed that they did.

Hugh knew nothing about the sick room, and he was afraid to touch her, but she began to convulse with fever and appeared to be in pain. He called for Emory and sent him to fetch more ice as he attempted to bathe her forehead and arms with cold cloths as he had seen Miss Craig do.

By the time Emory returned, Hugh was about to send for Miss Craig, but he hated to disturb her much-needed rest. He felt very out of his element. There was a bottle of some medicament on the night-stand and he did not know if he should give her anything. Why had he not thought to ask?

Letty cried out in pain and grabbed at her right side, but still she did not wake. How would she react when she awoke to strangers?

"Emory, what do I do?"

"I have no idea, your Grace." He glanced up and his valet looked as though he were about to swoon.

"Leave me, Emory. You are of no use to me on the floor." The valet hurriedly escaped, the coward.

Hugh continued to bathe Letty, though she was now shaking despite feeling hot to the touch. Did that mean her fever was break-ing? He paced around the room twice, debating whether to wake Miss Craig.

Letty screamed again and the decision was made for him, as Miss Craig came running into the room whilst attempting to pull a wrap around herself.

"Thank God!" Hugh exclaimed.

"What has happened?" she asked, worry etched on her face.

"She keeps crying out in pain and is shaking. I have been applying ice to her, but it does not seem to help."

Maili came closer to look.

"Should I stop the ice?" he asked.

"No, she still burns with fever."

"Her side seems to pain her. Is there anything we can give?"

Maili gingerly felt Letty's abdomen with her hand, eliciting a cry of pain again from the girl.

"Should we give her this..." He picked up the bottle and read the label, "this Calomel?"

"I do not know. My papa thinks Calomel can be dangerous. How I wish he was here!"

"Then what can we give?"

"Where is the still room? I can see what there is. A saline draught or Peruvian bark might help the fever and pain."

He told her where to find the room. She would need to pass by where all of the sailors were being nursed, and if she were lost she could ask the servants the way.

"I will ask them if they need anything while I am there. I am certain those sailors are in as bad a condition themselves."

"Hurry back. I am at your mercy."

Miss Craig left and he said silent prayers of thanks that she did have her wits about her. She was more than capable in this situation— much more than his valet— and she had even swum out to try to rescue one of the sailors!

He could not imagine his mother doing anything of the sort, other than standing on the shore barking orders. He rather liked the idea of a woman unafraid to sully her hands if necessary. Not that he wanted her risking her neck ever again, but he was humbled by her willingness to save others.

Letty groaned again, bringing his mind back to the present. He dipped each of the cloths, which had already grown warm from her heat, in the cold water and place them around her body. It seemed to help settle her for the moment. But however would they survive three weeks of this?

~

Maili made her way quickly through the house towards where the sailors were. She could smell the sick room long before she reached it, and the wrenching sounds of their deep, wet coughs echoed throughout the long, marble hallways. She disliked the fact that the older retainers were the ones left to care for these extremely ill men. If only her papa were here to help! She did not trust this doctor and his nostrums.

She opened the door to the saloon quietly in case anyone was fortunate enough to sleep. She saw Mrs. Sizemore covering another body with a blanket and had to choke on a sob. It was not the time, she scolded herself, but would all of this be for naught?

Mrs. Sizemore caught sight of her and scurried over.

"Do you need something, miss?" she asked kindly.

"You have lost another?" Maili asked, even though she knew the answer.

The woman nodded. "I think he is better off now, the poor thing."

"I was on my way to the still room. Is there anything I can fetch for you?"

"I do not know what you will find there. We have had very little need of it, thankfully. If you have any notion of what would help, I would be glad of it."

"I will see what I can find, then."

She closed the door softly behind her and went through the kitchens to the small room nearby. It did not look as though the jars had been disturbed in an age. She began brushing away the layers of dust in an attempt to read the labels. Catriona would know what most of these things were for, but Maili was feeling very inept. After some minutes of searching, at last she found willow bark and Peruvian bark. She did not know how old the tinctures were but they would have to suffice. She went into the kitchen and began to prepare the draught. At least she had done this before with Catriona's supervision. The Duke would be wondering where she was, but it could not be helped. While she was waiting for the medicines to distil, she prepared some barley water, because no one else had time. They needed a dozen more hands to nurse all these people, yet they only had five, two of whom should have been pensioned off, and the others were useless. Maili had learned some of the requirements of nursing in the orphanage; she had been the youngest then, but she remembered everybody had all had to do their share. She would find other things for the valet to do. Not everyone was suited to sickrooms, as her papa had often said to her.

Armed with Peruvian bark and saline draughts, she left the barley water simmering over the fire and went to deliver some of the vials to Mrs. Sizemore so that lady might try to relieve some of the sailors' fevers and pains. She then made her way back up to the yellow bedchamber to visit Letty.

The look on the Duke's face when she opened the door would have been comical had the girl not been so sick. It portrayed gratefulness and desperation at the same time.

The woman was trying to sit up on the bed and he was attempting to push her back down. Her eyes were staring at nothing and she was furiously trying to pick away something she thought to be on her leg.

Maili hurried to the bedside and placed her vials on the table.

"Letty," she said calmly. No response. She looked to the Duke. "She has reached the delirium stage already. I believe she is further advanced in the course than we thought."

"Is this a good or a bad thing?" he asked, a fierce wrinkle between his brows.

"It will not last as long as we feared," she replied. "If they make it through the third week of fever they are expected to live."

He closed his eyes and let out a breath. "How many weeks has she been like this?"

"I would guess, two. Letty!" Maili said to the lady as she held the saline draught to her lips. "You must drink this. It will help you to feel better."

Letty finally looked at her but was obviously very confused, to judge by the glare she gave her.

"Drink," Maili commanded.

Letty obeyed, taking most of the draught without complaint. Maili was relieved because she did not know what she would have done otherwise.

She finally looked over to the Duke, who was staring at her.

"I am forever in your debt, Miss Craig."

She gave him a look of amusement. "Maili," she corrected as she laid Letty back down and tucked a sheet around her. She dipped the cloth back in the ice water and placed it on her forehead.

"I have been trying to calm her down for this last half-hour and you walk in and accomplish it in less than five minutes."

"I have some experience, despite the wish that I did not." She chuckled. "Growing up in an orphanage and a physician's household bestows that on you."

"I expect it will." He sat slowly and slouched on the chair behind him.

Maili began to feel self-conscious when she felt his eyes upon her. This crisis had only proved how different she was from the ladies of the *ton*—and she realized she did care very much what he thought. However, she could do no differently. She would never be one to stand by and watch as others suffered or struggled. She would always say more than she ought, and she would always do things she ought not. Tears began to fill her eyes and she blinked them away. She was tired and becoming melodramatic. Never did she have any expectations of a match as grand as a Duke, but she had come to care very much for this man, and she felt her own ache inside because of it.

She set the last cloth down and walked towards the window. It was going to be a long wait until they were released from quarantine. Would it be possible to avoid him? Seeing him vulnerable and in close proximity would be more than she could bear.

"You should go back to sleep," she heard him say behind her. She shut her eyes to steel herself to be strong.

"I do not think I could," she replied. "She should rest for a few hours until the dose wears off. Why do you not take some rest? I will wake you if anything changes."

From the corner of her eye she glimpsed his hand come up to touch her, but she did not move.

He hesitated and she saw him let his hand drop. He stood there another moment and then decided to leave.

The tears spilled over and she did not try to stop them. It would only make it worse.

"Please God, send my papa soon."

CHAPTER 21

$\mathcal{D}$ays and nights, nights and days. They had become one and the same to Maili. She was exhausted. It had been several days, at least, since that fateful wreck. There had been no word from her Uncle David, and only a short note of apology from her aunt when Lady Brennan had sent over her belongings.

There had also been little change in Letty, and Maili was beginning to fear the girl would never recover. Her high fever seemed to have subsided when the bouts of delirium had, but Maili knew little else about typhoid, and the doctor had not returned again.

The sailors seemed improved, though they were much too weak to return to the sea—if they had a ship to return to, that was. All in all, life was dreary at Gracemere. Maili did not think it could be long until her papa arrived for her, and that gave her something to look forward to. She had seen the Duke again, of course, since they had taken turns staying with Letty, but something had changed between the two of them. She no longer felt the relationship growing—if anything, it had ceased. Or perhaps she had imagined it altogether. This was no time for fantastical romances anyway, when so many lives were still in peril. She did miss the sense of friendship she had felt, but it was easy to feel despair when you were on the brink of exhaustion, with no relief in sight and no one to share it with. She fell into the armchair near Letty's bed, feeling quite sorry for herself.

"I remember you."

Maili looked up and around the room before realizing it was Letty who had spoken.

"Did you say you remembered me?"

"You were here before and helped me."

"I have been with you for several days."

She shook her head. "No, before. When I was a child. I always remembered the beautiful lady with the red hair and the kind smile."

"You must be thinking of my mother. She died in a carriage accident, probably not long after that. My name is Maili."

"I am sorry to hear it. You look exactly as I remember her. I am Letty."

"Where have you been living?"

"I have lived in the West Indies since leaving England," she explained, though her voice was weak.

"Who did you live with? Were they on the ship?"

The woman looked away. "No. I watched my papa die. That is why I had to leave."

The door opened and the Duke looked in. His face registered Letty's consciousness and he glanced at Maili. She smiled and nodded to him.

"Letty, this is the Duke of Cavenray."

"You must be my half-brother, then."

He walked over to her and took her hand. "I am happy to meet you at last, sister. You have been very ill and I was beginning to fear for you."

"I am very tired," she said sleepily, "but I have wanted to see you again for all these years. It is most inconvenient to be ill."

"There will be time. I, too, have many questions I would like answered."

"I should leave the two of you to become reacquainted," Maili said. She stood up, feeling she was intruding.

"Please do not go," Letty said, pleading with her pale, blue-grey eyes which made her greatly resemble the Duke, even though the shade was lighter.

Maili looked at the Duke, who nodded for her to stay, so she cautiously sat down again.

"You look very much like our papa as I remember him," Letty said, not shy about looking him over. "I was quite young, but I remember his dark hair and your eyes."

"Have you been happy, then?" he asked.

"Yes, David has brought me up as his sister. He could not have been kinder to me, were I his own flesh and blood."

"I am relieved to hear it."

Maili thought of her own situation and her estimation of her Uncle David grew. Had they been very mistaken about him? How could one man have two such completely conflicting characters?

"I was brought up on a sugar plantation on the island of Barbados. It is warm and sunny all year there," Letty said softly.

"How different you will find it here. It rains more days than not, and the air can be quite brisk. We learn to cherish the sun when we see it."

"Do you remember me from the summer Papa died?" Letty asked.

The Duke looked to be thinking back, his eyes distant, searching old memories.

"I was small, but I never did forget. I picked apples with you and you carried me on your shoulders when I grew tired."

"That was you? I thought you were Cook's little one," he said in disbelief.

"My mother could not keep me, so Papa hid me here. I was ever so happy when he came to visit," she said wistfully. "You were so kind to play with me."

"I do not know why I did not see it then, or why Father never told me about you. I would have made sure…" He looked away, as though to compose himself. Maili's own throat swelled with emotion.

Letty reached out and placed her hands on his. "You did not know, and you were grieving yourself."

"You are very gracious. I still do not understand why David chose to take you away from me. I would have looked after you. He told me when he left you here after the wreck that you were the difference between life and death to him. Do you know what he meant?"

She nodded. "Our plantation was destroyed by a great storm last autumn. If it had not been for that, we might never have returned. David did very well for himself there—I believe he is a wealthy man now. However, when he lived here before, he was involved in some dishonourable acts, and from what I gather, they were smuggling." She looked at him for confirmation.

The Duke nodded and she continued.

"He said things got out of hand, that someone he was involved with became greedy. Papa found out and intended to stop it. I was on the beach one night with my father, taking a walk, when two men confronted him—one of them was David. He told me to run back to the house."

"Oh, no," Maili whispered. She could feel what was coming.

Tears streamed down Letty's face and she was clearly reliving that night. The Duke sat on the bed next to her and began to stroke her hand.

"I did not go back. I saw everything. The other man hit Papa and held him under the water. David tried to stop him, but could not."

The Duke sat still for a while, stunned into silence.

"David ran to the house to get help, but instead, found me. It was too late for Papa, and David feared the man would attack me next, so he took me and ran away."

The Duke pulled Letty into his arms. "My poor sister. What you have been through!"

"At least we have each other now." She sounded desperately weary.

"As well as three more brothers you have yet to meet."

"Three?" She looked astonished.

"Indeed. You shall meet them in good time. For now, I intend to protect you and help David seek out this other man. He would not tell me who he was, but I suspect he is trying to find a way to bring him to justice. David has become the scapegoat in all of this, I am afraid."

Letty yawned loudly.

"You need to rest for now. I fear you may be required to testify in order to clear David's name, and for that it is imperative no one knows you are here and who you are."

She nodded as her eyes began to close.

"Welcome home, sister." He leaned over and placed a soft kiss on her forehead.

~

Hugh made to leave and remembered Miss Craig was still sitting there in a chair. He turned and motioned for her to follow him. He still could not quite comprehend all Letty had told him, but Miss Craig was similarly involved. His emotions were fragile, but it did not mean he could walk away and leave her here. She had been through hell alongside him for the past fortnight and deserved more than he was capable of giving her.

He took her hand and began to walk. He could not think properly, yet her presence comforted him. There was a sitting room adjoining his apartment and he opened the door and pulled her inside. It seemed selfish to need her so much, especially at a time like this. They stood facing each other and he could not bring himself to speak. Those soft gray eyes seemed to understand his silent pleas and she stepped forward and wrapped her arms around him. He inhaled deeply of her soft red curls and felt himself relax. With her in his arms, he at once felt everything would surely work out.

How could he adequately express to her how he felt? There was a murderer to catch, yet their time together was growing short. He could not allow her to leave, not knowing his deep admiration for her, but eloquent words failed him at a time such as this.

Desperately he took her face in his hands and began to kiss her. Inelegantly, their lips met in a fury of expression, her passion seeming to match his. He was mad to touch her, to show her his affection and how he needed her. They kissed until they were both panting; needing no words, they slowed to a tender touching of lips. He touched his forehead to hers and she joined him in laughing at their frenzied display. Was it possible she could feel the same as he? She had become essential to his happiness and comfort; could he ever be the same to her? Hugh felt anything but silly, despite the laughter. He felt a deep, intense longing and knew he must rein himself in before he lost all control. It was easy to lose his bearings when reality as he knew it had shattered around him. One thing was clear to him, however: he wanted her as his help-meet for the rest of his days.

She was looking at him with those large silver-grey eyes; they were full of passion, her lips swollen from his kisses. He had to bite back a groan of frustration. He wanted to declare his love now, but it was not the time.

"I must go and meet with Lieutenant James of the Revenue. I would very much like to finish this conversation later."

"Conversation?" she asked with open amusement.

"There are also words which need to be said. You are, of course, quite free to leave, but I would beg for your assistance with my sister a little while longer. I want someone here with her at all times. She is not yet strong enough to defend herself, and I do not know who to trust."

"Of course. I did not nurse her through this only to see her murdered," Maili added with wry humour. "Besides, my father has not arrived to escort me home to Scotland, yet. I cannot say I relish returning to Brantley until he comes."

Could she mean what he hoped she did? He would treasure the thought until the time he could ask her properly.

"Do you know how to use a gun?"

"Naturally," she answered with a mischievous grin.

The devil himself could not have been more tempted to toss propriety to the wind when she looked at him like that. He cleared his throat and tried to concentrate.

"I will have Emory bring one to you. Keep it with you at all times."

"If that is your wish."

"Will you promise to be careful? I cannot know how events will transpire, and whoever is behind this whole business is not afraid to kill two more females should they be in his way."

163

"I will do my best."

"I think it wisest not to mention Letty's presence to anyone else, not even your aunt and uncle, should they decide to visit."

"I think that unlikely, but I will not mention her to anyone."

He stepped close again and gently ran his finger down her check before placing one more tender kiss to her lips.

"See that you do. I want you waiting here for me when I return."

He gave her one last look, full of meaning, willing her to feel as he did before forcing himself to leave her.

Lieutenant James awaited him in the study. The Revenue Officer was shifting his weight from one foot to the other and appeared anxious.

"My apologies for keeping you waiting," Hugh said as he walked through the door and closed it behind him. "What have you discovered?"

"Lord Brennan knows where Captain Deuce is hiding. He is ready to move and arrest him."

"And he has enough evidence against him?" Hugh asked suspiciously.

"I saw him at the wreck with my own eyes!" The man raised his voice uncharacteristically.

"I was also there; will you arrest me?"

The man did not answer but he was clenching his jaw with anger.

"Did you see Deuce actively smuggling goods? No, you did not. He was assisting the passengers, as was I."

"Lord Brennan is the magistrate. If he orders me to arrest him then I shall do my duty."

"And who will be made to look the fool when there is no evidence? Will it be my word against yours?"

Hugh let the man consider that for a few moments.

"Some new information has come to my attention and I believe there is someone else behind all of this. Someone who is willing to use Deuce to his advantage. How much of what happened before did anyone prove him to have his hand in? When he went into exile, he was a convenient rogue to blame everything on," Hugh explained.

"Do you mean to tell me you think him innocent of all crimes?"

"I did not say that. I believe he has been involved in smuggling in times past, although I have no proof."

"Can you prove what you say? I do not answer to you, but Lord Brennan."

"I would argue against that. You answer to the Crown. The Crown is fully aware of what is happening here. I will make certain they know your orders came from me."

The Lieutenant was beginning to break out in beads of sweat on his forehead. He was fidgeting with his sword and rapping his hat against his thigh. "What if you are wrong, your Grace? There is a great deal at stake here."

"I am well aware what is at stake, Lieutenant. I do not have proof of who the mastermind is yet, but I have proof there is someone else other than Deuce behind this. I even have proof that he is not the villain he has been made out to be."

"What is this proof? Where is it to be found?"

"That I will not reveal until I have more information on the leader. Innocent persons, or shall I say more innocent persons, will lose their lives if we are careless."

"More? What do you mean?"

"This man killed my father," Hugh stated quietly.

"By Jove, that is a lofty charge! Was his death not ruled an accident?"

"Indeed. So, you see it has now become personal. However, we must remain awake on all fronts or we will be outmanoeuvred."

"Why has Deuce not come forward with this information before? I assume it is he who told you?"

"He was protecting someone, and in all probability, his own neck."

The Lieutenant looked to be assimilating all Hugh had said. His head was shaking and his gaze was uncertain.

"Your Grace. Do you realize it must be someone very powerful to have this hold over Deuce, if what you say is correct?"

"I have known Deuce since we were at school. I am very well

aware of who we are likely to be dealing with, and it is why I urge you to proceed with the utmost caution."

"Do you have a plan, your Grace?"

"I do, but it will require my speaking to him. Have you any idea where he is hiding himself?"

"I do not, Lord Brennan has not yet told me."

"Then play along with Lord Brennan's wishes for now, and keep me informed if he tells you to act. We do not know if he is being given orders, either. I have a hunch about Deuce's whereabouts. I will send word to you when I am ready."

The Lieutenant took a nervous breath. "As you say, your Grace." He clicked his heels together and made a bow.

Hugh watched until the officer mounted his horse and rode away down the drive.

"Emory!" He called for his valet, who was now filling in for any task not to do with the sickroom.

"Yes, your Grace."

"I must go out. Please see that no one enters this house without my permission. And see that Miss Craig has one of the pistols. You should keep one with you as well."

"Yes, your Grace." Emory stood tall and saluted.

Hugh shook his head. He did not have the energy even to rebuke his insolence today.

"Fetch me my coat and my hat."

"Yes, your Grace."

Hugh pulled on his gloves and strapped his pistol to his belt. He strolled to the kitchen and packed some bread and cold beef into a towel. Feeling extremely generous, he pulled a bottle of ale from the larder and met Emory at the door. The valet helped him into his coat, and pulling his hat on his head, Hugh set out for the folly.

CHAPTER 22

*H*ugh walked far enough around the folly to make sure no one was within earshot before he was satisfied and began the climb to the upper chamber. He was not surprised to find no sign of inhabitants when he arrived at the top. He walked to the hidden compartment and knocked.

"It is Cavenray," Hugh said quietly in case his voice carried. He still recalled the day he had overheard Deuce and Lady Brennan.

He heard a rustle behind the door and the lifting of the latch.

"I think we could have found you some accommodation within the house," Hugh remarked when he surveyed the rough-looking man before him.

"It is easier to come and go unremarked from here," Deuce explained.

Hugh handed him the food and ale he had brought. "For you. I suspected you might need some nourishment."

"I am much obliged. The fare has been scarce, though I have raided your larder a time or two," Deuce confessed, helping himself.

"Letty has broken the fever and is awake at last," Hugh said as Deuce ate.

"Thank Heavens," the other answered with relief.

"She enlightened me on a great many things, including the death of my father."

"It was most unfortunate. I should have told you, but I was young and I panicked. I was not exactly innocent and very likely would have taken the blame."

"I am grateful you protected her. I cannot change what is done."

"You are being uncommonly gracious. I know there has been no love lost between us in the past."

"It seems I wronged you," Hugh admitted.

"No, you did not. I was the scoundrel you thought me. However, it seems there was a small measure of goodness somewhere inside my miserable being, for I could not bear the children to suffer."

"Children?" Hugh asked, wondering what he had missed.

"I have said too much," Deuce declared. "I wish to handle this business myself. There is no sense involving anyone else. This is an old score I intend to settle on my own."

"Do not be ridiculous! It is my father he murdered!"

"And my good name," Deuce pointed out.

"Allow me to help you. It sounds as though you will need it."

"All these years away from England, I have dreamt of a way to catch him, to make him suffer." He held out his hands in a plea.

"You had best act quickly, then. The Revenue Officer just came to see me. He says Brennan has enough evidence and has ordered him to arrest you."

"I am not surprised. It is easy enough to produce evidence."

"Do you not think it is time to tell me who your illustrious partner is?"

"What was that?" Deuce whispered, ignoring Hugh's question.

"I did not hear anything."

"Quick, get inside!"

"No, you go. I would rather like to know who is come to my property uninvited."

He helped Deuce back into the hidden compartment and waited. The footsteps drew closer and Hugh braced himself for the unknown.

"Ah, Cavenray, when did you come to Westmorland?"

"Good day to you, Brennan. I just arrived for a holiday, only to find my house was volunteered to quarantine of a ship-load of passengers."

"You were not expected and have not been here in years," Brennan explained. "It seemed the simplest solution."

"My elderly retainers may not see it that way. What brings you to Gracemere?"

"I was sent word that a criminal might be hiding out here."

Hugh was sure his face must have evidenced his surprise.

"Yes, I must deal with such matters myself, on occasion. We do not have the Runners on every corner here in the country."

"I have seen no one about who is unexpected. I can be sure to send word. Who precisely are you looking for?"

"I doubt he is anyone you know. He has been in the East for well over a decade. He led a vicious smuggling gang and was exiled, but has now returned to disturb our peaceful shores once again."

"What is this notorious person's name?"

"He is known hereabouts as Captain Deuce."

"Does he have a beard, a peg leg and an eye patch?" Hugh asked, making light of the situation.

"He might well. I have not seen him in so long I might not recognize him."

"I will be certain to inform you immediately if I see any strangers."

"There is a possibility he is, at this moment, in your house under quarantine," Brennan remarked. "Though I did not see him on the beach the day of the wreck."

"I gather the ones who survived are improving, though I have not been in the sick room myself," he told him.

"Nor would I expect it. I would like to see the men before they are released, to question them."

"Of course. I will send word. Good day, Brennan." This conversation was growing tedious.

"Oh, and your Grace? Lady Brennan's niece is there. My lady will be wanting to know how Miss Craig does."

"I saw no ladies present. However, I was told only two male sailors had died, so I would assume she is well."

"Excellent. I am glad to hear it. I know Lady Brennan will be relieved. Good day."

Hugh waited until he saw Brennan exit the folly and walk away, back towards Brantley. He opened the door.

"The cat is out of the bag, I am afraid," he said with a heavy sigh.

"You did not have to do that," Deuce said. "I will have to face him sooner or later."

"I rather suspect sooner, but it is always best to do it on your terms."

"Precisely."

"Do you have a plan to catch the leader, then?"

"There is no way to do it other than lure him to me and fight him to the death."

"This is the nineteenth century, Deuce. Surely, we can discuss it as gentlemen? The man has to be a gentleman—someone with power— for there is no way to have this hold over you otherwise. Do you deny it?"

"I do not. However, there is nothing gentlemanly or civilized about the manner in which he operates. He simply kills anyone who defies him."

"Then a trap must be set where witnesses with equal power can stand against him."

"He is too clever. He will smell it a mile away."

"Make it irresistible," Hugh suggested. "Every human has at least one weakness he cannot completely conquer. What is the one thing he wants that only you can give him?"

"Other than my head on a silver platter?" Deuce asked derisively. "I can think of nothing other than pride. But he has been clever enough to make certain I would never be believed."

"I have an idea, but you will have to trust me."

~

"What do you mean, you doona have my daughter?" Lord Craig was having difficulty keeping his temper. He had not wanted Maili to come here to Brantley to stay with people who were practically strangers, and now they were telling him she was not here?

"I understand it looks very bad," Lady Brennan said. "There was a terrible shipwreck. She went out to help without telling me, or I would have insisted she stay here."

"Is Maili hurt?" Gavin was quickly losing patience.

"She is quite well. We had word today. She is at the neighbouring estate, Gracemere. The sailors were taken ill when they were washed ashore and she has been aiding them, the dear child."

"So how did she come to leave your care, Lady Brennan?" Gavin wanted answers.

"As I was saying, the sailors were ill, and the surgeon considered she had been exposed and needed to be quarantined."

"Quarantined from what? Why did you not keep her here? I canna believe what I am hearing!"

"She has been there for the past two weeks, helping to nurse the those who survived the wreck," Lady Brennan replied meekly.

"I trusted you to look after her. If anythin' at all happens to her, I will personally hold you and Lord Brennan responsible. Now which way is Gracemere?"

Gavin sat in the carriage fuming as he made the short drive to the next estate. He could call Brennan out for this, and Gavin was about the mildest man alive. He could not remember a time when he had been as angry as this.

He alighted from the carriage before it stopped and almost stamped up to the front door. A pompous-looking servant opened the door and looked down his nose at him.

"May I help you?"

"I am Lord Craig, here for my daughter, Miss Craig. Kindly show her to me *now*." The *now* was said with a venom Gavin had not known he possessed.

"I am sorry, my lord, but I have strict orders not to allow anyone in the house without his Grace's permission."

"I beg your pardon? Who is his Grace to hold my daughter hostage? I would speak with him this instant!"

"Therein lies the problem, my lord," the servant said, beginning to look acutely uncomfortable. "His Grace is not at home."

"And when do you expect him to return?" Gavin asked, trying not to eat the messenger.

"I could not say, my lord."

"Then send my daughter to me. At once."

The man was clearly struggling with conflicting emotions. "I suppose that would be acceptable."

"Unless you are holding her hostage, it deuced well is acceptable!"

"Would you care to wait on the terrace?" The man stepped outside and led him to a veranda overlooking the gardens. *Unbelievable*, Gavin grumbled. He paced the stones, growing more furious by the minute.

"Papa!" Maili exclaimed as she hurtled straight towards him. He braced himself for the very welcome hug.

"Maili! I was beginning to think I would never find you."

"Oh, Papa, what stories I have to tell you," she said, sitting on a bench.

"I can only imagine, from the limited amount Lady Brennan told me. You do look tired. Have they been taking proper care of you?"

"As best anyone could. There were only five of us and we began with nine ill patients. We do not count the valet who cannot abide the sick room."

"And how many have you left?"

"Seven," she said quietly. "The two who died had doubtless taken in a lot of water during the shipwreck. Others drowned before we could save them." ·

"Has the fever passed?"

"I believe so. Our final patient seems to have broken through this morning. The others are still very weak."

"It will be a little while longer before we know if you are to come down with it."

"I know," she whispered. "But I was careful, as you taught me to be."

"So, how did this come to pass? Are your aunt and uncle as incompetent as I take them to be? How could they have left you here alone with only four servants? And with nine sailors—even if they were ill? I cannot fathom what came over them!"

"Everything turned out all right, Papa. I was glad to be able to help."

He smiled at her. "Of course you were. You could not escape medicine after all, could you?"

"I was glad for the little knowledge I managed to retain from you, Catriona and Seamus. Knowing how to prepare a saline draught and some Peruvian bark tincture proved quite useful."

"I imagine it did," he chuckled. "Now tell me, why is no one allowed in the house? Are they still afraid of the fever?"

"Well, the quarantine has not been rescinded yet, but that is not the main reason. It is a very long story and not entirely mine to tell."

"When will this Duke return? Has he been here the entire time? I do not believe your aunt was aware of this."

"She was not. He was on a repairing lease and did not wish it known he was here. We met each other quite by accident one day, so I already knew. I was quite surprised to see his house appropriated without his consent. However, it was already done and he decided not to make a fuss."

"That was gracious of him. Who is this Duke?"

"Cavenray," Maili mumbled.

"The bachelor Duke who was courting your new sister, Christelle?"

"Yes," Maili whispered. "I was afraid this would happen. It is not what you think, Papa. We have been caring for the sick and taking turns to rest. Please do not force any proposals upon him, for he is honourable and I would not wish it."

"Maili, my dear child, if only it were so simple. If word leaked out…" He shook his head.

"I know, but we will see it does not. No one will hear of it as far as Craig. No one here even knows of his presence."

"We shall see what happens. Now, shall we gather together your belongings? The sooner we can be away, the less fodder for scandal."

"I cannot leave yet, Papa. I promised him I would look after someone."

"Is this someone still sick? Shall I have a look? That is, if the butler will allow me inside."

"Do not worry about Emory. He is the valet I mentioned. The Duke is trying to protect somebody. This is where the rest of the story begins. You may look at her but do not ask who she is."

"Maili, I canna like this," he warned her.

"I gave my word, Papa. But I do think it would be reassuring for you to assess the patients. The village surgeon has not returned since we arrived."

"Verra well, but I expect a full explanation when his Grace arrives."

Maili then led him up to see a young woman, and he agreed that she had passed through the fever. However, it would be some time before she regained her strength.

They next made a call on the main sick room, and the sailors appeared to be stronger than the young lady. Mrs. Sizemore and Watson, the old retainers, looked rather haggard and Gavin reassured them that the sailors were out of danger. He ordered them off to their own rest.

After that, Maili led him to the drawing room, and he could only imagine what the past two weeks had been like for her. He placed his arm around her and kissed her head.

"I am verra proud of you. I know you did not place yourself in the situation intentionally."

"And like most things, I did not think before I acted. It is my own fault."

"I wouldna trade your heart for anythin' in the world, lass. My only hope is we can leave here with your health *and* reputation intact."

"Your Grace!" Maili exclaimed when she saw the man standing in the corner of the room as they entered. Gavin had met Cavenray before, but they were not well acquainted.

"Lord Craig, welcome." The man held out his hand in greeting.

Gavin hesitated before taking it. "I canna say I am pleased to find my daughter in this situation."

"Papa, no! It was not his doing. The surgeon and Uncle Brennan are to blame, if it need be placed," Maili pleaded.

They ignored her.

"As you say. I would never have had her placed here. It was too late by the time I was apprised of it. Then the situation became more difficult. Perhaps you and I should remove it to the study and discuss this further in private."

"Would you mind checking Letty is comfortable?" the Duke asked Maili very casually, looking up. Gavin realized there was clearly more to the situation than either of them was telling him.

"We have just come from there and she was sleeping peacefully," Maili replied curtly. "Papa examined her and thinks she will make a full recovery. Now, what have you to say that I am not privy to?"

"Come now, lass. Let us speak," Gavin gently commanded. Maili thought for a moment before responding.

"Very well." She bobbed an irreverent curtsy and walked briskly from the room. Gavin wanted to laugh. He had missed her fiery temper.

"This way." The Duke indicated the hallway and led him to a study filled with books, a desk and comfortable leather chairs.

"I am afraid I might need your help," the Duke confessed, once they were seated.

"With Maili?" Gavin asked, trying not to grin.

"Yes, that will come later, with your permission, but there is something more pressing. We have a murderer in the vicinity who we need to catch."

"A murderer?" Gavin asked. He had dealt with a killer once and that was enough for a lifetime.

"The woman upstairs is my half-sister, and if this man knows she is alive then it is probable he will try to kill her. She was a passenger on the ship which was wrecked. Sir David Douglas had escaped with her many years ago, when she saw my father murdered by this man."

"Sir David Douglas. The uncle of my adopted children?"

"Indeed. He has been credited with many nefarious deeds, some of which he did commit. Of the worst of them, he appears to be innocent. The magistrate, Lord Brennan, has ordered his arrest. But first, we wish to use Douglas to lure the murderer out of hiding."

"Someone will be killed," Gavin said.

"Douglas is aware of this, but we can think of no other way. I believe the more of us with power who witness, the less likely this man is to get away."

Cavenray continued to fill Gavin in on the details and history of the smuggling gang and his father's murder.

"This is a horrid mess, but I agree, it must end now. Is the plan already in place?"

"It is. Douglas has requested a meeting on the beach tonight. I would prefer that your daughter and my sister be unaware of this circumstance."

"It would never do!" Gavin exclaimed. "Maili would be there with pistols firing!"

Humour lurked about the Duke's eyes. "Yes, I imagine she would."

CHAPTER 23

I believe they are planning something. They were entirely too quiet, and my papa never retires early," Maili said, fidgeting with the blue ribbon on her gown.

"I agree. Hugh kept checking his watch," Letty said.

"I would bet anything they are planning to confront the leader of the gang, but where and how?"

"Probably at the beach. Where else would be secluded and make for an easy escape?"

"I do not think it would be easy to get away. I would want a horse if I was planning on fleeing quickly," Maili said, recalling how difficult it had looked to row across the waves.

"I suppose so. I still think the beach would be more private than anywhere else around here."

"Hmm. I am not certain I agree. There are some pretty barren hills about."

"Perhaps it is a feeling inside. It is where they seemed to conduct their business before. He had no compunction about murdering my papa there."

"He must have no conscience whatsoever! They do not trust us to keep our heads." Maili pouted. "Perhaps with good reason; I do have a temper."

"I would only be a hindrance," Letty admitted plainly, "but what I would not give to see such a man brought to his knees! I owe years of nightmares to him!"

"I would think my papa, my uncle and your brother ought to be quite a force to be reckoned with against one man," Maili said thoughtfully. "But I still wish to watch."

"I cannot think of how. I am too weak to go so far."

"We need a bath chair. It is a chair with wheels and you can push a person about. However, I do not happen to have one at the moment," she noted with a sigh. "Wait! Emory could carry you! He may seem useless, but he has a very fine form, if you look closely," Maili added mischievously.

"You minx! I mean that as the highest form of praise!" Letty clarified with a twinkle in her eye.

Maili stood up to pull the bell.

"Yes, Miss Craig?" Emory asked when he entered. He stared at them both in astonishment. They were dressed in cloaks and boots and ready for the descent to the beach.

"Lady Letitia desires a walk down to the beach and needs your assistance," Maili answered with the sweetest smile she could muster.

Emory's pleasant smile faded. "I am afraid I cannot oblige, Lady Letitia. The Duke gave strict orders for no one to leave the house."

"Did he, indeed? This is the first I have heard of it." Maili was not surprised. "Since I am not a prisoner and was never forbidden to go outdoors, I do believe I will go anyway. Letty, shall we?"

"But you cannot! I was told to protect you no matter what, yet I was also told not to let anyone leave. If you go to the beach, Miss Craig, I will lose my position!"

"While I appreciate you are in a difficult situation, Emory, we are going. You therefore have a choice. You may go and protect us or you may stay here and guard the house. Either way, we will assure the Duke that you tried to do your duty."

The valet made a painful, screeching sound in his throat, which almost made Maili giggle. Letty began slowly walking to the door. Emory threw up his hands in surrender and lifted her into his arms.

As they reached the entrance hall, they heard the knocker fall on the door.

Emory made a sound of fright. "Quickly, hide!" he exclaimed.

Maili and Letty shielded themselves in the drawing room before Emory opened the door to see who was calling.

"May I help you?" he asked, mimicking a butler.

"I am Lady Brennan," the woman said breathlessly, at the same time checking over her shoulder. "I have come to see my niece. It is imperative that I speak with her!"

Maili stepped out into the vestibule. "What is the matter, Aunt? Is something wrong?"

"Oh, Maili! I do not know," she said, appearing flustered. There was a deep bruise across her cheek. "Lord Brennan and I argued, then Lord Craig arrived and was upset with me and I came to apologize. Were you on your way out?"

Maili did not know what to say. "I-I was going to take a walk with one of the passengers."

"Then I will walk with you. I will keep my distance if you are afraid for them."

"Her fever has passed. I do not think you are in any danger." she reassured her aunt. Emory was standing behind Lady Brennan, trying to signal to Maili. He was mouthing, 'No', and pulling his hand in a knife-like fashion across his throat. Maili was not concerned that her aunt was the killer.

"I was unaware that there were any females on board," her aunt said with a furrowed brow.

"Yes, she was taking passage. She was quite ill when she was brought here. One moment, and I will fetch her."

Maili went into the drawing room and whispered to Letty to keep her hood down about her face. Letty nodded and Maili signalled for Emory to assist her again.

They started to walk outside and Maili hoped she could get her aunt to leave by the time they reached the dividing path. It would be difficult to explain their errand to the beach at this time of night. "What has you upset, Aunt?"

"Your uncle came home in a state this afternoon. He was quite angry."

"My uncle was angry?" Maili had never seen him thus. However, she had seen him very little, in fact.

"I should not say such things. It is normal for men to lose their temper on occasion," Lady Brennan reasoned.

Maili had never seen her papa angry enough to hit anyone, and she was furious with Lord Brennan.

"Why was he upset?"

She was shaking her head. "I have already said too much. I should not turn you against him. He will settle down and everything will be well by the morning."

"Was it to do with the wreck? Did something happen with one of the prisoners?"

"It is my brother," she replied, clearly struggling with her confession. She looked behind her where Emory and Letty were trailing at a discreet distance. Maili slowed as they grew close to the path. They could not be having this discussion when they came upon the scene on the beach.

Maili whispered. "What has happened with my Uncle David?"

"Brennan is very upset with him. There is very old history between them. He never expected David to return to England."

"Is it because I am here?" Maili could not help but wonder.

"I believe it goes much deeper, I am afraid."

Emory drew closer with his burden and paused near them. He placed Letty on her feet and shook his arms.

"Perhaps we should turn back. The woman and servant are growing weak," Maili suggested. "She will catch a chill in this strong wind." It was growing cold and the winds were gusting with increasing strength.

"Mama?" Letty said then, the word lifting in enquiry.

Lady Brennan's face looked like she had seen a ghost in the moonlight.

"Who are you?" she whispered.

Letty lowered her hood and took a step closer.

Lady Brennan's shaking hand came to her mouth. "He told me you were dead," she said, her voice shaking. "He told me both of you died together!" she wailed.

"Shh, Aunt, I hear voices on the beach. We must not let them know we are here."

"My sweet, sweet child is alive!" Lady Brennan said lovingly as she touched Letty's face with her palm, and Letty grasped the trembling hand between her own. Maili could not believe what she was seeing and hearing. If Letty's mother was her aunt and her father was the old Duke, that meant...

"He lied to me all these years! He lied to me! Not one single day has passed that he has not reminded me of my sins and held it against me!" Her aunt began to cry.

"I am here now, Mama," Letty said calmly, trying to soothe Lady Brennan, who looked near delirium.

"Take her back to the house," her aunt ordered Emory. She began marching down to the beach.

Maili started to chase after her without looking to see what the other two were doing. Her aunt did not know about the murderer and would be killed if she ran into the middle of a fight.

Maili pulled her gun out and readied it.

❧

Hugh hated waiting. They were placed all around the cove—witnesses —ready to bring this horrible chapter to a close, one way or another. He hoped Deuce would be given a chance and would see that he did if he survived this.

He was certainly ready for the holiday he had intended.

Lord Craig was on the northern point, Lieutenant James was to the south, on Brennan's land, and Hugh was in a central position between the two. There were some officers in the water, even one hiding in Lord Brennan's skiff, should the man they awaited go for that means of escape. A few more men were waiting if he arrived on horseback, but Hugh really did not know what to expect. Deuce had handed him his Will before walking out into the sand, and Hugh felt as though a frog had lodged in his throat, knowing Deuce must feel he was facing an execution.

Douglas stood still while he waited, and Hugh could only admire his courage. Were he in this situation himself, he would surely be pacing from one end of the shore to the other.

At last, another man came strolling down the path between the two properties.

"Deuce."

"Brennan."

It was as Hugh had suspected. There was really no one else.

"I was beginning to wonder if you had lost your nerve," Deuce said.

"I think there is little to be said between us. You should not have returned," Brennan replied.

"I have plenty to say. Surely you can oblige me in this?"

"It matters not what you say, but if it relieves your conscience before you go to your eternal destination, by all means, speak, though no one else will hear you."

"This is a game to you. How many more lives have you taken since I left?"

"I do not know of what you speak," Brennan drawled.

"Have you forgotten about Cavenray and my brother's family?"

"They were both horrible accidents," the magistrate said dismissively.

"Was it a nice surprise to see Miss Craig in London?"

"I quickly surmised she knew nothing. A brainless simpleton, much like her mother." He answered as though he was bored.

"Be that as it may, it will not be long until people begin asking questions. Why did no one know they were alive? Who took them to the orphanage?"

"All trails lead back to you, Deuce."

"You tried to make certain of that while I was away. Of course, I took the children to the orphanage—before you could murder them like you did their parents. Thankfully, I happened upon the carriage wreck before you did. It was obvious the axle had been tampered with and it was no accident."

"It is a very fine story you tell, but you have no proof."

"And when you killed Cavenray, you had an audience. Were you aware there was another witness besides me?"

"One I will take care of when I finish with you. She would have been safe had you kept her in the Indies. Do you think I want to look at my wife's cuckold, who is the image of Cavenray?" Brennan aimed his gun straight at Deuce's chest and cocked it. "To all appearances, it would seem as if you quickly realized there was no way out and took your own life before the law came for you. Did you know there is a warrant out for your arrest? That you were to be taken before the assizes?"

"You may kill me now, but you will not escape this time. You have just confessed in front of a lofty crowd of your peers."

"I have confessed nothing," Brennan refuted.

"You lied to me!" Lady Brennan came rushing out onto the beach, shouting. Miss Craig was chasing her, a gun flailing in her hand.

"Annie, go home. Now!" Brennan commanded without looking at her.

"I will never listen to you again!" she screeched.

"If you care to watch your brother die, so be it. I did warn you," Brennan replied.

Before Hugh could sneak up behind Brennan, Lady Brennan grabbed Maili's gun from her and in a whirl of fury, turned and fired.

"Aunt, no!" Maili shouted.

Multiple shots followed, and Hugh threw himself towards Maili. It was no more than a few seconds of chaos, but to Hugh it stretched into what felt like an eternity as he awaited the outcome to this culmination of Brennan's reign. He heard cries, followed by shouting, and then, unfortunately, someone was rolling him away from Miss Craig's body. It was a great shame, he decided.

"Cavenray?" A worried Scottish brogue hovered in the air above his face, asking the unspoken question. Then came Emory, gushing and snivelling, and sounding like a *ton* mama in need of smelling salts.

"Maili?" Hugh asked, trying to open his eyes and focus his gaze.

"I am here." Then he saw her face come in to view. "Are you harmed?" she asked with her eyes narrowed, searching him for injuries, if only by the light of the moon.

He smiled. "I think I swooned," he laughed, before he remembered himself and started to sit up.

"Easy now," Lord Craig said and he helped him upright. "It appears the back of your head was grazed with a bullet. I will need to examine it more closely in the light."

Hugh reached back to feel his head and felt something wet and sticky on his hand.

"You saved my daughter, though, so I will be eternally grateful to you for this scratch," Lord Craig said quietly.

Hugh looked up to see Maili's beautiful face looking down at him, and she wiped at her eyes. Reaching down, she tore a strip from her petticoat and wrapped the makeshift bandage around his head. He recalled the situation and looked around to see the aftermath of the gun battle. Lieutenant James was standing over Brennan's body, and Letty and Deuce were kneeling over Lady Brennan.

"Oh, no. She spared her brother only to..."

"I think she is still alive!" Deuce bellowed.

Lord Craig hurried to the lady and bent over her to see if she could be helped. Maili sat down next to him and took his hand as they watched her papa's life-saving efforts.

"I need light," Lord Craig announced.

A rush of men and horses swarmed down the hill and within minutes they had removed Lady Brennan to the house, where she could be tended.

Hugh and Maili sat on the sand, watching quietly as the Lieutenant dealt with Brennan's body.

"We should have that wound seen to," she finally said.

"Not yet." He pulled her closer and rested her head on his shoulder. "Maili, I am not a man to be effusive with words."

"I know," she whispered.

"I am attempting to declare myself to you; must you be impudent now?"

"Forgive me. Please do go on." She looked up at him and he could see her love for him by the moonlight reflecting in her eyes.

"Very well. I wish for you to be my wife." He would no longer delay what he should have said long ago. He had almost lost the chance.

She was still looking up at him, and he grew concerned.

"Say something, Maili."

"I think you will feel differently come morning. You have had a dreadful fright tonight. When you can think rationally, you will regret such words."

"You mean to tell me I do not know my own feelings? That I have not desired you since I first saw you in London? That my feelings for you have not grown every day until they are bursting with my love for you? If you cannot return my regard, then say so, but do not tell me I do not know my own heart." He looked at her intently, awaiting her response.

"I am astonished beyond measure," she answered, still returning his gaze. "From the first, I never imagined you felt anything but disdain for me. You courted Lady Christelle and scarcely had a word or glance for me. We have developed a kinship from our time here, 'tis true, but I told myself the kisses were nothing more than a man with natural desires for female companionship. But when we return to life as normal, you will find I am not suitable to be a duchess."

Hugh wanted to howl in frustration. He had thought those very things she now tossed in his face, and knew himself to have been woefully mistaken. "Do you know why I came to Gracemere?"

"To enjoy some peace and respite?"

He scoffed. "My dear girl, I came in an attempt to erase you from my every thought. Do you think that every time I was in your presence this Season I was pining for Christelle? Quite the opposite was true, in fact."

"Yet you were prepared to offer for her."

"It never came to the point, and never would have done. I could

185

not do it. She was my mother's choice, and when I came to London, I had little care for who my bride might be."

"But I was not up to snuff."

He made to object but she held her hand up.

"I know it, you need not say it. If I had been, would you have not offered for me then? Yet you felt the need to escape to the country to forget?"

She moved away and stood up, shaking the sand from her skirts.

"You have been kind to me, and you saved my life tonight. I am eternally grateful to you. I think, however, in time you will find you agree with me."

"Will you take time to consider?" he asked as he also stood up and joined her for the return to the house.

"It will not change my answer," she said sadly.

"Can you honestly tell me you do not have any tender feeling for me? Could you not grow to love me, in time?" He was grovelling. Could she not feel what he did?

She began to cry and shook her head before hurrying on ahead of him to the house. He watched her go, feeling bereft. What else could he have done?

CHAPTER 24

*H*e loved her? Could it be true? Maili tried to think back to their time together in London, but it seemed a lifetime ago. She could not allow herself to be caught up in her own emotions. She must think of what was best for him. He must feel honour-bound to offer for her and was attempting to make the best of the situation. He was very convincing!

She was no fool, despite the way she seemed to behave a good deal of the time. She had seen the fine ladies of polite society, and she knew she did not compare. She had no desire to try, either, if truth be told. Of course she loved him. Who would not, once they knew him? How she had misjudged him, for he was nothing like the man she had assumed him to be. He was anything but the cold, pompous wretch she had taken him for! But that was why she could not hold him to her for propriety's sake.

He had been so earnest on the beach. She would savour those moments for the rest of her life. There would be no other hero for her. She did not think she could marry any other and hoped her parents would understand.

Reluctantly, she went back into the house. She needed to see how her aunt fared. If anyone was capable of saving Lady Brennan, it was Papa.

Maili was grateful he had arrived, and hoped that God would spare her aunt this time. What she must have suffered at the hands of that barbarian, Brennan! How deceived they had been by him! If what Sir David said was true, he had killed her parents and tried to kill all of them.

She walked slowly by the dining room, where they had laid Lady Brennan on the table. Her papa was trying to dislodge a bullet from her spine. She still had a small chance, then. Maili knew she would be little help and so went on to her bedroom, where she gave in to the pain and sobbed. She could not sort through her feelings properly. Perhaps she should heed her own advice and not try to make life-altering decisions when she was in a state of shock.

Some hours later, she stirred to feel a hand on her arm. She had fallen asleep atop her coverlet, still wearing her blood-spattered dress from the evening before. It was already morning; she could see by dawn's light creeping through the window.

"Papa. Have you been up all night?" she asked, rubbing her eyes.

He nodded. "The bullet was lodged in a very difficult position in her spine."

"Did she...?" Maili could not bring herself to say the word allowed.

"She is still fighting, lass, but I do not know for how long. She is very weak from losing so much blood, and I do not know if she will be able to use her legs again."

Maili knew her face had wrinkled into an ugly mess but she could not control it.

"Why, Papa?" she wept.

He took her in his arms and held her tight. He was used to seeing such things and she did not know how he could always be so strong. She sobbed again and wondered where all of this emotion was kept. It felt like years and years of hurting was all escaping at once.

She inhaled a few rapid breaths as her tears eased, and pulled back to look at her father. She smiled half-heartedly at him. "Was anyone else injured?"

"Most of the bullets seemed to land in Brennan. Your Uncle David and the Duke both had some minor wounds but should heal nicely."

Maili suspected her father was about to break into a speech, since he now grew quiet. He had that look in his eye.

"Maili?" She did not wish to meet his gaze. He was going to say something she did not want to hear.

"Yes, Papa." She glanced at him and then back down at her hands on her lap.

"Cavenray was very distraught when at last I was able to treat his head wound."

"Was it worse than we feared? I should have stayed to look at it in the light," she said, at once growing worried.

"No, it is not the head scratch that I refer to."

She closed her eyes and took a deep breath. Was the Duke going to use her papa against her now?

"Papa, I do not wish to force him. He only says these things from honour."

"No, lass. Those are not the words of a man duty-bound."

"How can you be certain? Did he tell you what he said?"

"I do not need to hear the words, Maili. Allow me to say, as a man who feels the same about your mama, you would be a fool to let him go."

"I would embarrass him, Papa! I am not suited to be a duchess. Did you see me in London? It was a comedy to rival Mrs. Jordan!"

"Of course I did. I saw a beautiful young lady, full of life. Perhaps the *ton* is a bit more stilted than you, but should it not be up to Cavenray to decide if you would suit him? If he is happy with you as his duchess, then why should you walk away and make both of you miserable?"

"I do not think it is so simple, Papa."

"Make it simple, Maili. I have never known you to give a fig for what others think of you. From the day I first saw you, I knew you were special. You were like this bright ray of light that refused to be hidden. Do not hide it now."

"Oh, Papa." She threw her arms around him again. Was he right? Could she be the wife Hugh needed? "It will not be easy."

"Nothing worth having ever is, lass. Now, go and put that poor man out of his misery and tell him you love him."

"Yes, Papa," Maili said with a shy smile. That was embarrassing, she thought, as she went to find the Duke. Would he still have her, or would she reach him before he came to his senses?

She caught sight of herself in the glass and stopped. She should at least change into a clean gown and brush her hair! She had not had a maid's attention in weeks, and it was a wonder the Duke could even consider her at all.

Lavender seemed the best choice for the sombre, yet joyous occasion. It was one of her favourite colours, but it was also a sign of loss. There would be no mourning Lord Brennan, but her aunt's life was in peril; learning of her parent's murder was sobering and she felt grief anew. Her hair was a lost cause, but she brushed it until it was silky and placed a matching ribbon around her head.

Maili went in search of the Duke, but he was nowhere to be found. The only place she had not looked was his apartments, and even she was not brazen enough to go there alone.

Beginning to lose her courage, her shoulders fell and she turned to walk away.

"I thought I detected your fragrance," he said from behind her. "Dare I hope you were coming to reassure yourself that I am still alive by the light of day?"

She turned and eyed him, one hand on her hip.

"That is rather presumptuous of you, sir. Perhaps I was taking the long way to my own room."

He raised his eyebrows at her and leaned against the doorpost. His gaze was warming her insides and she was certain she was flushing. Suddenly, she could not think of what she wanted to say. He was too distractingly handsome in his shirt-sleeves and with his hair dishevelled, even with a bandage wrapped around his head.

"Maili, come here."

Her feet began moving towards him, even though she was beginning to feel those unwelcome sensations of inadequacy again. She shook them away as he held his hand out to her.

"I have reconsidered," she said softly as she took his hand and looked up into his fathomless blue eyes. She swallowed hard.

"Have you?"

"Never." His face broke out into a grin and he pulled her into his arms. He kissed her forehead. "Soon this will be mine." He kissed her ear. "And this." He kissed her shoulder and then back to her lips. "And these." He trailed a few more kisses down her neck. "I really admire your neck. Have I told you? No? It will be mine, too."

Maili could not help but laugh.

"Soon," he continued.

"Not before the baby is born," she remarked.

"I beg your pardon?" He was looking at her, his expression a mixture of shock and puzzlement.

"Oh! My mama is expecting very soon. It is why my father came to fetch me now. You thought..."

"I most certainly did not. I would have remembered such a momentous event," he remarked casually as he proceeded to kiss her other ear.

"You certainly would!" she chastised as she pushed back and hit him on the arm.

"We had best go and inform your father, because I am suddenly an impatient man."

"You could return with us and we could be married at Castle Craig, in Scotland," she offered.

"But, my dearest, I have my heart set on a grand London wedding at St. George's. I intend the whole world should know that you chose me."

Maili could not believe her ears, but she no longer cared, for they and her heart now belonged to Hugh.

It had been an emotional day. The sailors had finally been released from quarantine at the direction of Lord Craig, whose medical expertise was felt to be superior to that of the village surgeon. Lady

Brennan was still alive, but was weak from the operation. It felt sacrosanct, but there Maili, Letty, David, Hugh and her papa were, sitting at the dining room table where she had lain the night before.

No one seemed to have an overly voracious appetite, for there still seemed to be so much left unsolved—at least Maili felt unsatisfied.

"Is something on your mind, Maili?" Lord Craig asked. "Your soup appears to be very well stirred."

She dropped her spoon. She had not realized she had been stirring so loud.

"Forgive me. I cannot stop feeling as though some of the pieces of this puzzle have been misplaced. There are many questions still left unanswered."

"Perhaps in time, Maili," her father replied.

"We are informal here tonight. I imagine you are not the only one with questions," Deuce said.

"Just so. You said you were in league with Lord Brennan in the beginning, which is when you became Captain Deuce and gained your reputation," Cavenray stated.

"That is correct. It began as a harmless smuggling operation, designed to supplement Brennan's estate and provide me with some funds to start a new life in the West Indies." He took a sip of his wine, then continued. "The villagers are ever pleased to have extra funds and drink, and there was little attention from the Revenue men in these parts. That was until Brennan raised the stakes. No one paid any heed until he decided to wreck ships."

Everyone had stopped eating and was listening with rapt attention.

"Why did you agree? Could you not have walked away then?" Letty asked.

"By that point, Brennan had something against every one of us. He was the magistrate, so he could easily create evidence and no one would question him."

Deuce paused for a few moments, as if going back in time. "The first wreck was lurid, even for me, who had come to think there was not a thing I could not do. I had become well acquainted with the most unsavoury characters when I began gambling at school. He expected us to deliberately lure ships onto the rocks and then kill all survivors, leaving no witnesses." Deuce swallowed hard. "But he made a mistake when one of the ships belonged to the Crown. Suddenly the authorities wanted someone's head."

"And Brennan was prepared to give them yours," Hugh added.

"As you say," Deuce agreed. "Everyone was here, looking for answers. My brother Nigel was suspicious from the start. He and your father, the old Duke, began to nose about and were starting to put two and two together."

"So he had the Duke killed," Lord Craig stated.

"No, he did it himself," Letty offered. "I saw everything. I remember it like it was yesterday," she said with her eyes closed.

Deuce reached over and held her hand.

"You were the witness. It was difficult to piece the story together from the conversation on the beach," Lord Craig said.

"I was also there and had run for help, but found Letty. It was the next day, as I was making my escape with her, that I realized the depths of his depravity. He had arranged for Nigel and his family to be killed in a carriage accident, except I came upon the scene first. Nigel and Margaret were dead, but the three children were still alive —though stunned and in shock. The axle had been sabotaged. It was a miracle they lived. I panicked and took them onward to Carlisle, from where I had intended to make my way to the nearest port, except I overheard someone at a posting house talking about the Alberfoyle Priory. It was to be a fancy orphanage, if you will."

"So you were transporting four children while trying to escape Brennan?" Hugh asked doubtfully.

"It is impossible to credit, I know."

"Why did you leave the others and take me?" Letty asked.

"I had no relationship with Seamus, Catriona and Maili—I was not considered a proper influence. I knew I could not take all four, and you had witnessed the murder. I knew if he found you, he would kill you, for certain. You also reminded him of his wife's infidelity. Shaming him in public with a duke before she had provided his own heirs was unthinkable to one such as Brennan. To him, his name meant everything."

"But something does not make sense. My aunt said the Duchess was jealous of the attention he gave my mother, Margaret."

"That explains a great deal to me," Hugh muttered.

"I could see why it would be confusing. My sister met the old duke and fell in love before she was married. Her betrothal to Brennan was made by our parents when she was in the cradle. Even after Anna discovered she was increasing, she begged Brennan to release her."

"But he refused, I gather," the Duke surmised.

"Which surprises none of us to hear," Maili grumbled.

"My parents could not afford the breach of contract, and they were furious with Anna for having an affair with a married man. They were grateful Brennan would still have her and save them from ruin. So, she was sent away to have the baby, then Brennan forced her to go to London that Season and have a large Society wedding immediately. He thought she could forget her child," he said disparagingly. "Whilst there, Margaret was the go-between for Anna and the old Duke, so the Duchess assumed he admired Margaret, yet she was only helping her friend make arrangements for their child."

"My poor mother," Letty whispered.

"Indeed. Brennan was not kind to her. He made her suffer for not choosing him. He was not pleased to discover the Duke was housing Letty at the neighbouring estate. I do not know if he was the spawn of Satan before she spurned him. Either way, he has joined his twin in hell now."

"My aunt's recovery will not be easy, but at least she has you returned to her," Maili said to Letty.

"I am thankful to be given another chance to know her," Letty responded gratefully, looking to Deuce and Lord Craig.

CHAPTER 25

*I*t seemed it had taken forever for this day to come. Hugh had joined Maili and Lord Craig on their return to the castle to await the birth of the next Craig bairn. It was not long in making its arrival. Lady Craig was delivered of a healthy, bonnie wee lass as the Scots liked to say.

One might naturally conclude that the wedding would be held not long after the happy event, but since Hugh insisted on having the nuptials in London in front of Society, he freely admitted it was his own fault he had to wait so long.

Three long months he had waited. He had driven from Scotland back to Cambridge, where he had prepared himself for a battle with his mother. He did not wish to injure her further and he had practiced what he should say to her for weeks. He was shown directly to her, in her sitting room, not long after he arrived.

"Mother."

"In charity with me now, are you? You have been gone the entire summer. I hope you are well rested," she added dryly as she glanced up from her embroidery.

"This summer was anything but restful, but it was very...productive."

"Do I wish to hear what you are going to tell me?"

He would not argue with her, but he must tell her the story without pitying her. "I arrived at Gracemere, only to find a gang of smugglers operating on my land."

"How inconvenient."

"I will not trouble to recount the entire story, but Lord Brennan was found to be the leader and was killed, in the end."

"I had heard some of what you say. It was all over the news sheets."

"I was there. It is a pitiful legacy he left behind. It was also discovered that Lady Brennan had a child by my father."

His mother's face was still and she refused to look at him.

"You did not know it was her, did you?" he asked, feeling oddly tender towards her.

"I knew there was someone," she said quietly.

"But you believed it was Margaret Douglas."

"Yes," she whispered.

"I am sorry you were hurt, Mother."

She continued to look away. "Do not feel sorry for me. He was always honest about his feelings. He did not mean to hurt me."

"I had thought you indifferent to him. It does not make it hurt less."

She inhaled deeply. He felt much more enlightened about his mother. He debated whether to tell her about Maili yet.

"You have found me out. Is there something else you wish to tell me?"

"Yes, but it can wait."

"Are you going to marry her?"

"How did you know?"

"You had that look in your eyes I used to see in your father's when he looked at her. You are correct in assuming I was jealous. Margaret Douglas was so striking that I assumed it was she. They were often together. I was jealous of that look, wishing just once he would look at me that way." She paused. "I did hold it against your betrothed."

"I believe she is unaware of this. I have never met anyone so kind-hearted or forgiving as Maili. I do hope you will give her a chance."

"It must be disappointing to know your mother is capable of such pettiness."

"It only makes you more human, Mother." He walked over to her and placed a hand on her shoulder. "I will only be disappointed if you do not come to love her as much as I do." He gave her shoulder a squeeze and left her to grieve in peace.

~

Frost had kissed the ground and roofs on the chilly December day which was to see Maili Craig become a duchess. The sun was shining bright on the cloudless morning, belying the fact that winter was come. Holly and mistletoe decorated every doorway and bannister, and the smell of wassail and spices wafted through the town house. Her family had all come, every last person. It was her favourite time of year—she felt blessed beyond measure.

Lady Ashbury was finally granted her wish of hosting a lavish society wedding, and she was making the most of it. Maili was terrified of what her grandmother had created, but she knew it meant the world to her and thus would bear it. She was sure she would cherish these moments—once they were behind her.

Lilly helped her into her gown, a creation designed by her new sister, Christelle. It suited her perfectly. It was a simple, high-waisted ivory silk confection, with a transparent overdress embroidered with tiny red roses. A matching red ribbon sat high above her waist and long white gloves almost met her dainty capped sleeves. Her curls were tamed into silky perfection, and crowned with the Ashbury tiara of a central large ruby surrounded by diamonds. Maili had thought the last excessive, but she was quickly told to hush and smile.

The time had finally come to leave for the church. She was trembling with fear at the thought of all of London's elite—mostly strangers—staring at her, wondering who was she to have snagged the bachelor Duke.

"You look perfect, lass," her papa said as she came down the stairs.

"I am terrified!" she confessed. "Can you see my legs wobbling? I am certain the entire congregation will hear my knees knock together like a woodpecker!"

Lord Craig laughed. "They will be hiding under your dress, at least."

"I am quite certain they will know, but I mean to smile and make them wonder."

He gave her hand a squeeze. "Your mama and I could not be prouder of you."

"I would not be here today if it were not for you. I will miss you and Mama. Why must I feel as though I am losing my family? I know I will be happy with him."

"It is a momentous day, and it is hard to leave those you love. However, it is not goodbye forever. You canna keep the Ashbury clan away, no matter how you try," he said with the familiar twinkle in his eye.

She laughed. "Very true."

The streets were lined with cheering crowds and she waved as they drove by in Lady Ashbury's infamous white carriage, pulled by a team of four white horses. Her grandmother had outfitted all of the grooms and the driver in red livery to complement Maili's dress.

"I cannot believe they are here to see me," she said in wonderment.

He smiled at her and squeezed her hand as the equipage pulled to a stop in front of the cathedral.

"It is time," he whispered.

The bells were ringing, the crowds were cheering, but all she could think of was the handsome Duke who was waiting for her at the other end of the aisle. It gave her courage.

She took her Papa's hand and walked up the steps as the doors were opened wide. For a moment, she panicked. She made the mistake of looking at the pews lined with unfamiliar faces. Why was she here? She did not belong.

"Smile, Maili, and doona look at anything but the handsome man waiting for you at the end of the aisle," her papa said perceptively.

Wise words.

She saw some of the decorations her grandmother had added to the church, though they were surprisingly simple and tasteful. Fresh garlands, red ribbons and tapers lined each pew. It smelled as if it were Christmas. However, the true gift awaited her at the altar. She was humbled by the love she saw reflected in his eyes as he watched her, and she soon forgot about the congregation.

The organ ceased and the Bishop cleared his throat.

Dearly beloved, we are gathered together here in the sight of God, and in the face of this congregation, to join together this Man and this Woman in holy Matrimony.

It was truly happening.

Wilt thou have this woman to thy wedded wife, to live together after God's ordinance in the holy estate of Matrimony? Wilt thou love her, comfort her, honour, and keep her in sickness and in health; and, forsaking all other, keep thee only unto her, so long as ye both shall live?

"I will," Hugh answered.

Wilt thou have this man to thy wedded husband, to live together after God's ordinance in the holy estate of Matrimony? Wilt thou obey him, and serve him, love, honour, and keep him in sickness and in health; and, forsaking all other, keep thee only unto him, so long as ye both shall live?

"I will," she heard her voice answer of its own volition.

"I, *Hugh Arthur Philip Dickerson*, take thee, *Maili Douglas Craig*, to my wedded wife, to have and to hold from this day forward, for better for worse, for richer for poorer, in sickness and in health, to love and to cherish, till death us do part, according to God's holy ordinance; and thereto I plight thee my troth."

"With this ring I thee wed, with my body I thee worship, and with all my worldly goods I thee endow: In the Name of the Father, and of the Son, and of the Holy Ghost. Amen."

Had ever words been more beautiful or more frightening, she wondered, as he recited them while gazing into her eyes and placing the Cavenray diamond on her finger.

Those whom God hath joined together let no man put asunder.

Forasmuch as Hugh and Maili have consented together in holy wedlock, and have witnessed the same before God and this company, and thereto have given and pledged their troth either to other, and have declared the same by giving and receiving of a Ring, and by joining of hands; I pronounce that they be Man and Wife together, In the Name of the Father, and of the Son, and of the Holy Ghost. Amen.

Maili stood there, frozen. It was done.

"Maili?" she heard Hugh say.

She looked up at him, dazed.

"I love you," he whispered.

She smiled. "I love you, too."

"Now we need to sign the register," he told her and began to lead her to the vestry. That done, they partook of Holy Communion before the Bishop led them in prayer, and then Hugh was escorting her down the nave through the smiling attendees.

The doors burst open before them, raining in rays of sunshine moments before they walked down the steps into showers of rice and seeds, through the cheering citizens hoping to get a glimpse of the Duke and Duchess.

Here was where Lady Ashbury had saved her extravagance for, and Maili wholeheartedly approved. The square had been roped off for dancing, and tables of Christmas-themed food had been set up for all to enjoy. There was wassail and ale aplenty, plum puddings and meat pies for the masses. Lady Ashbury's servants handed out the fare, and the Duke and Duchess greeted those who had come to share in their special day.

"May I have this dance, my Duchess?" Hugh stepped aside and held out his hand to her.

"I would be honoured," Maili said with a smile.

The crowd gathered around as Hugh led Maili into a fast version of a waltz, delighting the common people with an uncommon view of near royalty. None would forget this day, nor the charitable couple who had shared their wedding feast with them!

"We have only danced one other time," Hugh said.

"And as I recall, I wondered the entire dance why you had deigned to ask me, and at the very last ball of the Season!" she laughed.

He looked down at her with a scornful glare. "You shall not chastise me, today of all days."

"Very well. I was just as mistaken, for what it is worth," she said breathlessly as he whirled her around and around.

"Pray tell."

"I took you to be a cold-hearted, prideful beast."

"This was your opinion of me?"

"Quite," she admitted.

"Then I look forward to every minute of proving you wrong," he said as he stopped and pulled her close for a kiss she could feel tingling all the way down to her toes. The crowd roared with approval, and Maili could feel her cheeks flushing as Hugh finally drew away. He looked upward and, with a devilish wink and teasing grin, plucked a berry from the mistletoe before dipping his head again for another.

PREVIEW OF MOON AND STARS

*I*t was always someone else's wedding, Lady Charlotte Stanton thought as she stood outside on the terrace alone, looking up at the dark, starry night. She had reached the age where she could be as improper as she liked and people would only shake their heads and call her eccentric. Part of her wished it were true. In reality, she spent most of her evenings curled up with a Minerva Press novel, in front of a warm fire, and a few cats to keep her company. It was not a bad life. It was often preferable to having to interact superficially with humans who expected witty repartee.

Nevertheless, there were those times when even she craved touch —human touch—and wondered what it would feel like to be kissed and held in adoration by someone she loved. Jealousy was not the precise emotion she felt, but there had been scores of love matches amongst her family and friends, and she was perhaps, on occasion, envious. It did not lessen her joy and delight for them by any means.

Earlier that day she had witnessed the union of the Duke of Cavenray to Maili Craig. She was not directly related, but she had formed a friendship of kindred spirit with the bride on a visit to London in the spring. Maili, too, had always felt an outsider but had managed to find love. Charlotte stared up at the stars and could not help but wonder if there was more for her somewhere out there.

"Sometimes I think I have more in common with the moon and the stars than Polite Society," a deep baritone voice said from behind her, as if hearing her thoughts.

Charlotte managed not to flinch. She was unused to anyone seeking her company in dark places.

"Yes, I was raised amongst the *ton*, yet it is not often comfortable," she replied, still looking at the night sky.

"That is the last word I would use for it," he said as he came to stand next to her. He was so close she felt warmth radiating from him and smelt his scent of spice and pine. She was afraid to turn and look. She did not wish to ruin the moment with reality, yet the arm of his coat appeared to be well made, and his hands appeared to be strong.

They stood there in silent kinship, listening to the sounds of laughter and dancing coming from the ballroom.

"Would you care to dance?"

Charlotte did not answer. This man must be someone new in Town, someone who knew not who she was, or could not see her clearly in the moonlight. What did it matter? It was only a dance. One dance would change nothing.

She held her hand out to him and finally allowed herself to look up.

"Have we been introduced?" she asked lamely. She had never before seen this man, of that she was certain.

His light grey eyes twinkled in the moonlight, and they were looking at her—her!—flirtatiously. Crinkles formed at the edges of his eyes, indicating experience and maturity that made him more handsome when he smiled. It was devilish cruel that men were more striking with age.

"You know very well we have not," he answered.

He pulled her close—too close—and began to twirl her around. The moment was too intimate for mere words. Charlotte felt light and dainty for the first time ever as this man spun her around in his arms. She must be dreaming. It was a heady, delicious feeling as her pulse raced and her insides quivered.

When the music ceased, they stood there still, retaining the position of the dance as their breathing slowed. Charlotte was growing self-conscious as the man studied her.

"Am I to know your name?" she whispered.

He took her hand and brought it to his lips, sending shivers through her.

"Some things are better left unspoken, my lady."

AFTERWORD

Author's note: British spellings and grammar have been used in an effort to reflect what would have been done in the time period in which the novels are set. While I realize all words may not be exact, I hope you can appreciate the differences and effort made to be historically accurate while attempting to retain readability for the modern audience.

Thank you for reading *Ray of Light*. I hope you enjoyed it. If you did, please help other readers find this book:

1. This ebook is lendable, so send it to a friend who you think might like it so she or he can discover me, too.
2. Help other people find this book by writing a review.
3. Sign up for my new releases at www.Elizabethjohnsauthor.com, so you can find out about the next book as soon as it's available.
4. Come like my Facebook page

www.facebook.com/Elizabethjohnsauthor or follow on
Twitter @Ejohnsauthor or write to me at
elizabethjohnsauthor@gmail.com

ACKNOWLEDGMENTS

There are many, many people who have contributed to making my books possible.

My family, who deals with the idiosyncrasies of a writer's life that do not fit into a 9 to 5 work day.

Dad, who reads every single version before and after anyone else— that alone qualifies him for sainthood.

Wilette, who takes my visions and interprets them, making them into works of art people open in the first place.

Karen, Tina, Staci, Judy, and Kristiann who care about my stories enough to help me shape them before everyone else sees them.

Tessa and Heather who help me say what I mean to!

And to the readers who make all of this possible.

I am forever grateful to you all.

ABOUT THE AUTHOR

Like many writers, Elizabeth Johns was first an avid reader, though she was a reluctant convert. It was Jane Austen's clever wit and unique turn of phrase that hooked Johns when she was 'forced' to read Pride and Prejudice for a school assignment. She began writing when she ran out of her favourite author's books and decided to try her hand at crafting a Regency romance novel. Her journey into publishing began with the release of Surrender the Past, book one of the Loring-Abbott Series. Johns makes no pretensions to Austen's wit, but hopes readers will perhaps laugh and find some enjoyment in her writing.

Johns attributes much of her inspiration to her mother, a former English teacher. During their last summer together, Johns would sit on the porch swing and read her stories to her mother, who encouraged her to continue writing. Busy with multiple careers, including a professional job in the medical field, writing and mother of small children, Johns squeezes in time for reading whenever possible.

ALSO BY ELIZABETH JOHNS

Surrender the Past

Seasons of Change

Seeking Redemption

Shadows of Doubt

Second Dance

Through the Fire

Melting the Ice

With the Wind

First Impressions

Out of the Darkness

After the Rain

Made in the USA
Las Vegas, NV
25 July 2023